SHERLOCK HOLMES AND
THE MENACING MONK

- disturbing revelations from Britain's remote islands causing consternation in Scotland Yard, confusion along the corridors of Whitehall and panic on the streets of Whitechapel.

Allan Mitchell

Paperback ISBN 978-1-78705-045-7
ePub ISBN 978-1-78705-046-4
PDF ISBN 978-1-78705-047-1

Published in the UK by MX Publishing
335 Princess Park Manor, Royal Drive,
London, N11 3GX www.mxpublishing.co.uk

Cover design by Brian Belanger

INTRODUCTION

From the mind of Arthur Conan Doyle, ever inquisitive, ever exploratory, never quite satisfied, emerged a figure we came to know as a man of unique abilities – unique, not so much in the fact of each individual facet of his character, but unique in the strength that each of those facets had in its development and unique in the power of the combinations each formed with others. We all, as he would repeatedly assert, possess the same senses but most of us fail to use the capacities of our minds to recognise what we perceive for what it is and what it means. Part extrovert, part introvert, both man of his time and social misfit, Sherlock Holmes presented an enigma – a man, at the same time amazingly adroit yet extremely annoying, demanding of himself yet impatient with and often dismissive of others. The circumstances of his extraordinary meeting with John Watson were as fortuitous as they were coincidental, two characters inhabiting different worlds brought together by a mutual friend who just happened to meet with both on the very same day they were seeking shared accommodation. But was it coincidence, or was it fate? It was certainly far more than fiction.

On first encountering Sherlock Holmes, John Watson had been downcast – a man of action reduced to a feeble and fumbling idler trying desperately to recover his former life, a reason to live, even to exist. His medical knowledge was sound, his background was solid, but his confidence was shattered as much as had been the bone in his shoulder upon receiving his fateful wound at Maiwand, disabling but not so much as his almost succumbing to the ravages of the Enteric Fever he contracted while convalescing at Peshawar.

It was John Watson's good fortune, as it has been ours as readers of the exploits he came to describe, to meet such a man as Holmes and find that he and Watson complimented each other with the skills and strengths each brought to a partnership whose fame was to blossom in their creator's time, never to wilt and die, only to grow in strength despite the passage of time, changes in writing styles, advances in detection methodologies and revolutions in forensic analysis. Successive generations have shared and enjoyed Holmes' and Watson's adventures in the days of Britain's industrial, geographical, commercial and naval supremacy by being able to feel they were part of the story and part of the team as felons were pursued and problems were solved by the use of Holmes' enhanced powers of observation and deduction, ably, though exasperatingly, kept in focus through the unfailing efforts of John Watson, M.D..

We, too, in modern times, find a sense of reassurance in the partnership of Holmes and Watson – we find a chance for order amidst the chaos which surrounds us and hope for those who choose the hard and noble road of honest effort on the surface of the sunlit Earth and not the deceitful and treacherous track followed by the felon lurking in the shadow. Their stories glorify the success of those battling adversity and injustice and view any positive outcome for the malefactor as an unfortunate but temporary aberration, something to be overcome in time by the vigilant and virtuous.

There have been many cases denied to Watson's pen in the interest of an innocent party whose exposure might have led to severe embarrassment, even ruin, were the facts of such a case ever to come before the Public. The very fact that Sherlock Holmes can act outside the control and constraints of officialdom gives him the ability to use his considerable discretion when it comes to what and to whom he tells of that which he has uncovered. He has, at times, acted as both judge and jury when feeling that justice has been sufficiently served and that further action might inflict undue harm upon the innocent, or that the guilty party has shown sincere remorse for undertaking actions under extreme duress. That a case should be seen for its entirety of cause and consequence is something for which the Great Sleuth would give his wholehearted support. Though this remarkable man acts primarily to keep his ever-active mind diverted from the drudgery of the everyday world, he is none-the-less a man of principle ever-ready to risk both life and limb to render impotent the evil-doer and the miscreant. Ability, justice and compassion are the three sturdy pillars of his personal world and, holding firm and true as they do against all adversity, they constitute the very essence of the very essential Sherlock Holmes.

CONTENTS

SHERLOCK HOLMES
AND THE MENACING MONK

THE RIPPER

The dread and revulsion at the outrages of that fiend of nineteenth century London's ill-lit neighbourhoods, Jack the Ripper, named so by a hyperbole-ridden press excited by the prospect of horrific stories driving up sales indefinitely, brought home the horror of the lawless streets and revealed the depths of depravity to which some humans can descend. Whether there was one fiend acting alone, whether that fiend was male or female, whether that horror held high office or whether that beast was known but deemed too extreme an embarrassment to the highest in the land should his, or her, identity be disclosed, are questions for which there is no absolutely reliable response, no definitive authoritative answer. The questions, however, still echo through public media unimaginable at the time of the dreadful events, even though the nineteenth century has long passed and the twentieth has spilled over into the twenty-first with graphic imagery of atrocities on a gigantic scale and in real time.

That the name of Sherlock Holmes is not to be found in the authorized accounts of the vile murders should come as no surprise to those conversant with his dilemmas vis-a-vis the official agencies, but it is unthinkable that the Great Sleuth would not have been involved, invited or not, in the investigation of such outrageous crimes.

As Watson makes no mention of such investigations in his famous discourses, there can be but two possibilities – either Sherlock Holmes independently determined the identity of the perpetrator of the dastardly crimes and kept mute on the matter as there was no possibility of their repetition, or he reported his discoveries to officialdom and was convinced to hold both his hand and his tongue as revelation of the identity of the Whitechapel fiend might do untold damage to persons of supreme significance. Prior to his involvement, however, the Great Sleuth, in desperation and frustration at sitting idly at Baker Street, threw down his newspaper with its sensation-filled headlines and said to his friend, John Watson ....

"I confess that the whole of the city's gone mad
With the fear that this fiend, that most pitiless cad,
Will continue his rampage of violent death
Causing many to render a terminal breath."

"I just can't understand why Lestrade hasn't called.
He'll be out of his depth but, also, quite appalled
That the fiend, that foul demon of Whitechapel's lanes,
Hasn't yet been arrested – my patience just wanes."

"I cannot form a theory – I don't have the facts
Which I need – I have so many useful contacts
Which I cannot make use of in these dire times
To assist the Police come to grips with these crimes."

"I've been warned off in language explicit and firm
And can only sit here in our lodgings and squirm
Like a worm on some hook but with no fish in sight -
To be cast in the waters would give me delight."

"Be that as it may, My Good Friend, but reflect
On the fate of a worm on a hook in respect
Of the fish it is tempting." teased Watson, *"You won't*
Fare much better than it, so I would suggest 'don't'."

"But I'm idle and useless, my mind needs release
From a state of inaction or else it will cease
To be able to function as well as it should."
Replied Sherlock to Watson, *"I'd help if I could."*

"Can your brother assist? He could well be a boon
To a man such as you – it would not be too soon
To approach him." asked Watson, in manner alarmed,
"Surely he wouldn't want any more women harmed."

"He surely could spare a few minutes, at least,
For his brother, to discuss this Whitechapel beast
And to recommend you as an agent, informal,
To Scotland Yard for all these acts so abnormal."

"Mycroft is tight-lipped – he'll not utter a thing
On the Whitechapel matters." Holmes said with a ring
Of despondence on being left out of the hunt -
He described his exclusion in words rather blunt.

"It is not in his province and not his affair,
He declares, though he does say he'll often despair
Of the lack of success enjoyed by Scotland Yard -
He says catching the murderer shouldn't be hard."

"Well, it seems that it is!" Watson said with disdain,
"And the Whitechapel citizens ought to complain
That all stops are not pulled to bring things to an end.
That Mycroft would sit still, I cannot comprehend."

"Yes. I feel that way also but his hands are tied,
So he claims." agreed Sherlock, who many times tried
To get those special agents Mycroft keeps on tap
To use all of their powers to set up a trap.

"Lestrade and his bloodhounds are up and away
And are chasing a quarry who just will not play
To the tune of the hunter – I hope I am wrong
But, it seems, with this quarry, they're playing along."

"It feels, I declare, they don't want this fiend caught
Even though all Whitechapel is hopelessly fraught
With the fear that the killings will go on until
Jack the Ripper has run out of victims to kill."

"Holmes, you have used it, that terrible name.
You have said that it was an incredible shame
That the newspapers glorify murderers, thus."
Reprimanded John Watson, *"That name's not for us."*.

"That is so," Holmes replied, *"but the fact is quite clear*
Those in London, and further, express a great fear
Of this fiend and require a well-fitting name -
I, too, feel that fear - I assign them no blame."

"But why do the authorities close every door?
I have paced back and forth over many a floor
Just to offer whatever small help I might be -
It is almost as though they're suspicious of me."

"Holmes, that's impossible. There isn't any
Less likely than you as the Beast – you've brought many
To justice by using your special technique."
Erupted John Watson, *"You're simply unique."*

"Perhaps that's the problem – sometimes my success
Has placed persons, official, under some duress."
Replied Sherlock, *"Perhaps I'm regarded by some*
As a threat to them gaining a favoured outcome."

"Or perhaps some regard me a likely suspect,
As a person of interest though cannot detect
Any evidence to justify my arrest -
Lestrade doesn't want me and he is their best."

"It's been said, more than once, I'm always on the spot
Of those crimes, most unusual, guessing the plot
With such ease, it would seem, that some say I'm behind
All those criminal acts of sensational kind"

"But those who would say that forget I was called
To assist the Police when their efforts had stalled
Many times from a lack of imagination
Or, more often, an absence of inclination."

"Inclination to do what is clearly required.
Do they fear what I am just because I'm inspired
To seek truth, absolute, from a world filled with lies?
In the cold face of logic, this jealousy flies."

"It's just jealousy, rampant, for what I've achieved
Many times when I've shown the Police what's believed
To be true, absolutely, as wholly unsound,
And the truth, underlying, so often have found."

"It's the newspapers, Watson, that stand to make most
Of an outrage committed – they brazenly host
Such conjecture extreme and embellish the facts
To make people read more of those scandalous acts."

"It's good business to them, circulation increases,
So any attempt to be accurate ceases
As editors find that the Public demands
More and greater sensation be placed in their hands."

"It is they, the newspapers, which should be decried
As the more likely agents of crime – they are tied
To a system of excess that's quite overblown.
How do we know The Ripper's not one of their own?"

"You can't think that is so!" uttered Watson, distressed
At the way that his friend seemed completely obsessed
With the notion that he wasn't granted the trust
Which he thought he deserved, *"That's a little unjust."*

"I know newspaper editors can be annoying
And can be perceived to, at times, be deploying
The basest of methods quite hard to defend,
But they do put the spotlight on failure, My Friend."

"Do they make up the news and not simply report it?
If a fact is too bland, do they simply distort it
To make something from it which doesn't exist?
They do, and all know it – but, still, they persist."

"It is one of those quandaries of modern life -
If the newspapers didn't exist there'd be, rife
And unknown to the Public, gross actions unjust
In those great institutions in which we place trust."

"Just the fact we have scandals reported at times
When those editors show up despicable crimes
By those holding high office, shows us that we need
Our newspapers quite free to expose every deed."

"I can think of our nation as so many teams
Placed in harness, of sorts, pulling all of our dreams
At a nice steady pace, but there are times, instead,
When a spirited horse must be given its head."

"That's the thing about spirit – it shouldn't be crushed,
Not in horses; and newspapers shouldn't be hushed
If we want them to tell us what we need to know -
So, some latitude on them, we have to bestow."

"That latitude," Sherlock replied, *"has to be*
Within limits, My Friend, for so often have we
Seen them turn it to licence attacking those who
Are constrained by the truth, as we now see them do."

"If good men of repute can be openly mocked
Then I don't see why people are readily shocked
When those men take no chances in matters of Law -
For some, being ridiculed is the last straw."

"A policeman's constrained by the orders he's given
By those set above him when actions have driven
Those people of office to put into action
A plan which will hopefully bring satisfaction."

"The official detectives must do what they're told.
If they don't, they can find themselves walking a cold
And quite miserable beat over cobble and tar -
They have latitude, too, but it doesn't go far."

"If only they'd call me, invite me to help -
I'd be off and I'd soon have that miserable whelp
In a cage looking forward to paying the price
For surrendering to his despicable vice."

Sherlock paced back and forth in his Baker Street flat,
Watson, ever his friend, standing there with his hat
And his coat at the ready should Sherlock decide
To go forth and, The Ripper, a challenge provide.

"We must both act together, alone will not do,
Because those who'd refute your great skills are apt to
Say that you are the one who'd committed these acts
Quite regardless of all indisputable facts."

"Sherlock, My Friend, on this point, I insist.
It would be a great folly for you to resist
My support and assistance – where you go, I must
Be seen there alongside you – you know this, I trust."

Sherlock nodded agreement but he remained mute
On the matter for some time – he could not dispute
There was need for swift action but also restraint -
Himself, with all pertinent facts, he'd acquaint.

He had read all the papers, the graphic reports
Of the gross mutilations, the claims of all sorts
Claiming intimate knowledge of who was the one
To have killed all those women and why it was done.

He was sick of the way the reports had been given
Such eager attention – his great mind had striven
To gather the facts without trimming or garnish -
"With embellishment, truth is the first thing to tarnish."

He would need to access the reports now denied
To himself and the Public – for days he had tried
To be given the chance to unleash his potential -
He was tired of being so inconsequential.

"I must have the facts, otherwise I am blind
To the ways of this monster – Lestrade is the kind
Of detective who writes down all that he can see
And normally with me, with those facts, he is free."

"He's been told, I believe, to keep me at arm's length
But I pray that the man exercises that strength
And resolve that he has as a good man and true
To allow me a look at each pertinent clue."

"Can I ask you, John Watson, to go on a quest
And see if there is some way you're able to wrest
From the clutches, official, those facts that I need?
Can I ask you to do that with consummate speed?"

Watson heard what was asked but delayed his reply
For he knew that his friend was the sort who might try
To divert him away from his actions and go
On his own – Watson struggled for *"Yes"* or for *"No"*.

He knew well enough that his friend was the sort
Who would often go off without any support
Or with even a single word of explanation -
But now if he did so, he'd get condemnation.

"Of course I will, Sherlock – I'll go right away
But I have to insist that, right here, you must stay
Till the time I return with the items you need."
Replied Watson, *"I warn you, my words you must heed."*

"If you go off alone, you must know it's the end
Of our dealings, Sherlock, and although you're a friend,
I refuse to continue our work if your trust
Doesn't stretch to respect – to wait for me, you must."

Holmes heard what he said and he knew it to be
Watson's ultimatum on the great trust that he
Had built up in a friendship whose one single flaw
Was that he, Sherlock Holmes, to himself, was a law.

"I will give you my word as a most sincere friend
That I'll stay in these rooms, though I will not pretend
I'm not anxious to get on the trail of The Ripper -
I'll just smoke some tobacco I have in this slipper."

"That will give me the chance to review what I know
Even though there is not much I have that will show
Me the way to the mind of this killer at large -
For now, My Dear Watson, you are in full charge."

THE YARD

Taking leave of his friend, Doctor Watson proceeded
To locate Lestrade to get what Sherlock needed
If only Sherlock, to his word, would stay true -
Watson well knew his friend when pursuing a clue.

But Sherlock would hold fast to his word, in this case,
For he knew that Lestrade had been hard on the chase
And that Watson must temper his objections, blunt,
Or they both would be trampled by those in the hunt.

Scotland Yard would resent interest uninvited
Especially from someone who'd get as excited
As Sherlock when acting to stop being bored -
As often as not, he would just be ignored.

But if he pressed the point when he hadn't been asked
To assist, he'd discover that anyone tasked
With the job of detection could resent intrusion
And be led to express an unfriendly allusion.

For many's the time an official detective
Felt pressed to say *"No!"* with expressive invective
When pestered by Sherlock on one vital fact -
Of all Sherlock's qualities, one wasn't tact.

Lestrade knew that the Doctor was not prone to fits
When denied what he wanted - those omitted bits
Of a puzzle which ought not to be given unless
This was sanctioned by orders exact and express.

He also knew Watson had patience and tact
And would not run off waving an unconfirmed fact
At his friend, Sherlock Holmes – he'd cooperate fully
Whereas Sherlock, at oft times, could come on the bully.

Scotland Yard had its systems, procedures one must
Follow fully with patience to generate trust
With those persons, official, one had to approach
On those sensitive matters one needed to broach.

It was crucial for any official detective
To follow procedures if he'd be effective
In bringing to trial a felon he'd caught -
With firm rules of evidence, Courts were all fraught.

This dilemma, of course, Sherlock would overlook
And, as often as not, when it suited he shook
Off the need for restraint that policemen must show -
Break the Law, just a little, for things he must know.

He did not need to worry with evidence rules.
He did not have to linger in Court vestibules
To be called to be badgered on all things he did
Bringing felons to Justice, the streets to be rid.

He could just be himself, do the things that he must,
Though the Law might declare that his acts were unjust
Should those acts come to light, then a Judge's decree
Could be that all the felons he caught would go free.

Sherlock Holmes, the loose cannon, could fire at will
While official policemen, the plodding Old Bill,
Had to stand by their guns until ordered to act -
At Court, all their evidence must stay intact.

With these factors in mind, Watson felt that he could
Ask Inspector Lestrade if there were things he would
Be prepared to divulge from the files, official -
The facts he and Holmes had were too superficial.

Appointments were useless - Lestrade could, for a day,
Perhaps more, from his office be off and away
Chasing clues to detect, chasing people to grill,
And, of such interruptions, he would have his fill.

But if he just appeared, he must be well prepared
To wait, ever so patiently, as if ensnared
By his desperate need for those facts under guard
By the forces of Law deep within Scotland Yard.

He might wait for an hour or even a day,
Perhaps two if Lestrade had been called far away
To chase up any lead, any clue to the name
Of the one who was bringing Police into shame.

To be seen to do nothing was fuel for the fire
Of Public Opinion although he would tire
Of having to check on each mischievous note -
Each one must be checked though with success remote.

Watson knew he would not be the first one in line
To be seen by Lestrade who might simply decline
To see any more people who claimed to know where
Jack the Ripper was hiding and who hid him there.

So he'd just have to wait till Lestrade had the time
And the inclination to discuss what was prime
In minds of the nation and share what he could -
Watson had to stay patient and vowed that he would.

Many hours he sat there with thoughts running wild -
Thoughts of further atrocities shaking his mild
Ordered world to the depths of its utmost foundation.
He could not conceive of the fiend's motivation.

But Lestrade was delayed, as detectives might be
On a case quite as complex as any that he,
In his varied career, could have ever expected -
His failure, so far, left him rather dejected.

Dejected, he was, but determined he stayed
For he was of the type who would be quite dismayed
If a man of The Yard would give up on a case -
That would be, for that man and The Yard, a disgrace.

Watson, too, was the type who would stand at his post
And await what might come with a patience that most
Would not ever believe could be managed by one
Who could write about what he and Sherlock had done.

Quick to act, he could be, but right now he was bound
To keep watch at The Yard till Lestrade had been found
And persuaded to show him all collated facts
Of the Whitechapel murders, those most dreadful acts.

Gregson sauntered on in – it was mid-afternoon.
John Watson thought that it would be none-too-soon
To approach him and ask when Lestrade would be back.
Gregson said, *"Well, that really depends on Old Jack."*

"Old Jack! Jack the Ripper! How flippant we seem."
Watson sharply retorted, *"We're giving esteem
To a fellow who rates nothing less than the rope.
I declare, with these names, I'm unable to cope."*

*"Well, Doctor, we must call him something, you know.
Everyone in Whitechapel would like us to show
Him the steps to the gallows."* Gregson answered back,
"It is they who are calling the monster Old Jack."

*"And the Press, don't forget, started all of this off.
In the papers, the fellow, they say is a toff
Or an aristocrat or a Royal gone mad -
Whatever the truth, we're all made to look bad."*

*"We've been warned against talking to Sherlock, as he,
Quite as likely as not, would take action that we
In The Yard wouldn't countenance, so we desist.
Sherlock Holmes, Dr Watson, is crossed from our list."*

"But Gregson," said Watson, *"his powers are such
That his eye, in an instant, sees ever so much
More than you or I could – he's a bloodhound for facts
And, in London, he has the most useful contacts."*

Gregson answered in earnest, *"Good Doctor, believe
Me when I say that I wish that someone would relieve
Me of all the restraints set to keep me in check -
I'd have Old Jack locked up tight in no time, By Heck."*

"Sherlock Holmes, as a bloodhound, can follow a clue
That so many can't see – I will pay him his due -
But a bloodhound is used as a part of a team
While your Mr Holmes can make Scotland Yard scream."

"If he'd stay on a leash till his master says 'Go'
He might well be an asset, but we must say 'No'
To his habit of chasing the choicest of game
When we're after a fox – Jack, to give it a name."

"I admit," said the Doctor, *"that Holmes can, at times,*
Be completely obsessive when looking at crimes
And will often forget that the forces of Law
Are restrained by its Statutes – it's his major flaw."

"But a hound which is held on a leash has to run
Free of all such restraints, now and then, having fun
Chasing game of all manner to hone up its skills.
And what good is a hound if can't lead to kills?"

Just then, as he said it, Lestrade came on in
And he said, *"Dr Watson, your argument's thin*
For we're not chasing game for amusement or sport.
We would only use Holmes as a final resort."

"We have used him before and, great use, he has been
But when it's been reported The Yard has been seen
As inept as your stories have always depicted
Us all, with stupidity, grossly afflicted."

"I can take that, myself, though it does at time cut
Rather deep for I hold him a friend of sorts, but
My superiors scream when they see in The Strand
How the Force is depicted as useless and bland."

"I do know why you're here and I wish I could say
'Help us out' but there has been, on this very day,
Yet another foul murder, the fifth one, to date.
One more innocent woman has met a cruel fate."

"I have come from the scene and I tell you I've not,
In my days on the Force, seen such horrors to blot
Out that faith in most people I've found hard to quell -
Such a monster, however, tells me we're in Hell."

"Our man with his camera couldn't proceed
With his job taking photographs – he felt the need
To be violently ill just outside in the lane.
He could not go back in; it would drive him insane."

"He's seen all kinds of murders, and bodies galore,
But the gross mutilations, the stench and the gore
In the room sent him off to regather his mind
And he's, normally, not of the least squeamish kind."

"We had to get somebody else for the task.
And so Brown from the morgue we proceeded to ask
For his help in the matter – to this he agreed.
His work makes him tougher than most of our breed."

"You've seen bloody battles, Watson, I suspect
But, an innocent woman, we're there to protect.
And she might not be such as might sup with the Queen
But she valued her life and, to keep it, was keen."

"To be murdered and butchered by this monster Jack
Is atrocious – I'd take him and then give him back
To the woman's relations, her closest of friends,
And let them do whatever they'd think made amends."

"Well, I'd be sorely tempted to do so, I fear,
But my duty with prisoners, all, is made clear
By the rules which I follow, though some may be bent
By a few, though it's only a minor percent."

"But your friend, Mr Holmes, he bends so many laws
While pursuing a problem, officialdom's claws
Had been close to his throat, but I managed to save
Him by saying I'll get Sherlock Holmes to behave."

"And, then, what do I get? Only more of the same;
And you write it all up as if it's just a game
To be played for the readers who covet your tales
And the income derived from the Strands extra sales."

"Come into my office, we'll wait until Brown
Can develop his pictures – he'll bring them on down
And I'll show you the horror of Whitechapel's nights.
It's a horror on par with the worst battle sights."

"I've been blasted from every direction there is.
The Commissioner even said to me that his
Little curly haired Spaniel could search out a clue
So much better than I could – I told him 'That's true'."

"He just roared and said 'Go out and capture this beast
Or the hounds of the Press will have you for a feast
When I throw you out bodily – get the man caught
Or your future within Scotland Yard will be naught'."

"All the folks in Whitechapel jeer at me and shout,
'Get Old Jack to the gallows or go and get out
And let somebody in who might know what to do.'
You're hiding somebody - we'd like to know who."

"And the Press has been at me, they're certainly hounds.
What they write isn't true, it is way out of bounds
For they want more sensation and someone to blame,
But it's they who deserve the lion's share of the shame."

"I would not be surprised to discover Old Jack
Isn't paid by the Press to remove all the slack
In the newspaper sales which had been quite low -
There isn't a standard they'd not stoop below."

"That's just what Holmes said." replied Watson who saw
That down onto Lestrade would soon drop the last straw
Which would, as goes the fable, at last break the back
Of this stress-laden camel – because of Old Jack.

"He did?" Lestrade queried, surprise on his face.
"I thought he would say that it was a disgrace
That I hadn't yet caught this man, evil and sly,
And if he was in charge, he would like to know why."

"Well," answered Watson, *"he's likely to say*
That about everybody he meets every day,
Most especially me when he can't find a clue
And a crime's resolution is way overdue."

"If he can be of help in this horrid affair,
He has so much to offer, you know, with his flair
For observing those things to which we are quite blind.
As a hunter of clues, he is one of a kind."

Inspector Lestrade well knew this to be true
For, in spite of five murders, no definite clue
To the reason behind them or who had committed
Such acts had been found – this had to be admitted.

"I declare, Dr Watson, I would like his help.
My superiors, though, would kick me like some whelp
If they ever found out I had let the man see
Evidence against their most explicit decree."

"Perhaps, if he assures me, and you guarantee
That the man will behave, I might just let him see
All our files on the crimes, but don't give him his head -
If he goes to Whitechapel, it's he who'll be dead."

Just as Watson had gotten Lestrade to relent
Just a little, a figure exhausted and spent
Rang the bell of Two-Twenty-One-B Baker Street -
Mrs Hudson emerged, a new client to greet.

From above he detected the sweet haunting sound
Of a strange melody, unknown to him, profound
And yet rather beautiful, poignant and deep -
Violins were not heard in a friary's keep.

"It's someone for you, Mr Holmes." she would yell
And then say to the visitor, *"Go up and tell*
Mr Holmes of your business – the head of the stairs.
Bang hard on the door, he's been playing his airs."

Holmes opened the door and to his great surprise,
Standing, right there before him, a man in the guise
Of an old hooded friar spoke these words, sublime:
"Mister Holmes, I'd be grateful for some of your time."

THE FRIAR

The old friar looked down unprepared to engage
Sherlock Holmes, eye to eye, fearing he might enrage
The world's foremost detective with what he must tell -
He seemed to have more fear of Holmes than of Hell.

Sherlock said, "*My Good Friar, come in and tell all,*
For you've gone to much trouble and come far to call
On this humble detective in these fearful times -
I presume you have news of these terrible crimes."

The old friar then entered and looked 'round the room
And the words that he spoke were like echoes of doom:
"*I have prayed for this world, Mr Holmes, but I fear*
That my prayers aren't enough for the Lord's noble ear."

"*I come here out of shame,*" the old friar confided,
"*And I fear that our order will soon be derided*
For what one, perhaps more, of my brothers have done -
If somebody can help me, I'm told you're the one."

"*I have told the Police – they just sent me away*
And declared that I'm mad and perhaps I might stay
With my fellows in Bedlam. Somebody must listen."
Welling up in his eyes, tears of terror would glisten.

"*I'm a man who, to peace, has determined to yield -*
Not a fool, nor a coward, but faith is my shield
And my God is my witness, my guide, and my rock -
The crimes in this city come as a great shock."

"*By the power of prayer, my good brothers exist*
And, avoiding temptations, we choose to persist
With a life that is simple, austere one might say.
Great evil is what makes me come here this day."

"The Beast is about – right among us he walks
Seeking those who show weakness - he patiently stalks
Anyone who shows promise or evil intent
Urging them to commit the worst deeds he'd invent."

Sherlock patiently listened - his visitor talked
About worries and terrors and fitfully walked
Without saying precisely why he took the time
To engage Sherlock Holmes, foremost fighter of crime.

Sherlock said, when the friar's emotion diminished
And the panic displayed in his ramblings had finished,
"Good Friar, I see that you're at your wit's end
So, to gather your thoughts, is what I'd recommend."

"Your faith's of a strength which is so hard to find
But I'd say, though it may seem a little unkind,
That your habit's no armour against evil's wiles -
Only courage protects us against all it guiles."

"So, take courage, My Friend, and sit down near the fire.
Tell me what's on your mind and what you might desire
Of this humble detective to calm any fears -
Speak up, My Good Friar, Sherlock Holmes is all ears."

The old friar sank into Holmes' comfortable seat
And accepted a goblet of a strong liquor, neat,
Which he sipped most discretely, discipline was his code
Though he felt like he'd either succumb or explode.

"Thank you, indeed, Mr Holmes, you're a breath
Of fresh air in this city, these dark streets of death."
Said the friar, relieved that he hadn't passed out,
"I've a great need to tell what my mission's about."

"But how did you know, from afar, I had come?
Did the Police inform you that I might have some
Information to give on those dastardly crimes
Which took place in this city in these evil times?"

"I can see from your habit," the Great Sleuth replied,
"From the weave of its cloth and the way that it's tied
And its texture, so coarse and so rough and severe -
You have chosen a life ascetic and austere."

"That is true, Mr Holmes," said this guest, in reply,
"It is not false humility which makes us try
To avoid excess comfort in clothes that we wear
But we do, to reduce it to function, all swear."

"Be that as it may," Holmes continued to say,
"There are no habits like it except far away
On the bleakest of outposts a person might find,
Outposts where someone might indeed meet his mind."

"You are rather articulate, that I can tell,
And your vocabulary is first-rate as well,
But you falter when starting to speak, as one might
When arising to speak while beset by stage-fight."

"This is no criticism, just what I've observed.
You're unpractised in talking, not one bit unnerved
When expressing opinion – this would, I suggest,
Point toward vows of silence observed with some zest."

"Your habit, your speech, and a northern accent
Tell me that you are cloistered with rules to prevent
Excess talking between all your colleagues unless
There is something to cause you some major distress."

"There are few places known to myself where a man
Such as you might withdraw to and live out his span
Full of prayer and reflection, and this has suggested
Our northernmost islands – remote, uncongested."

"I would say, from the Orkneys, you've travelled to find
Answers to a dilemma of troubling kind.
It is based, you have said, on these Whitechapel acts
But there's more to your visit so let me have facts."

"It is true, Mr Holmes," said the friar, released
From the tension he felt, *"my long silence has ceased*
Since a trio of friars left some months ago
After having been given a definite 'No!'."

"That was 'No' to a question of change in our ways,
From reflection and prayer on to outward displays
Of aggression toward anyone who'd transgress
Holy Writ – this was troubling I must confess."

"You are right that all talk is restricted so we
Can direct all our thoughts to On-High so that He
Might direct His compassion to those who deserve
Divine help in their struggles, the Beast to unnerve."

"But the Orkneys, it's not, Mr Holmes, though nearby.
On the island of Yell in the Shetlands, we try
To reach out with our minds to that Kingdom Eternal -
We must look deep within to depress the external."

"Just once in each year we may venture outside,
In a manner of speaking. Our rules do provide
For one man, wise and trusted, the tidings convey
From the world that we left to, God's good words, obey."

"He will leave for a week, travel wide though not far
In his quest to keep up with the news, popular,
From the town and the city, the port and the farm,
To know what has befallen, for good or for harm."

"He returns and will give, in one hour, the news
Of the world on the outside. We discuss our views
For one hour thereafter, in tones quite restrained,
Our vow to stay silent relaxed then sustained."

"That man has been me for the past several years
And I freely admit what I saw brought the tears
To my eyes more than once, for the marvels I saw
Stood stark, side by side, with outrages quite raw."

"There were people still hungry within the Empire,
People with outlooks depressing and dire.
Men full of anger you'd not wish to meet,
Women and children forced onto the street."

Here, the friar went silent, though not from his vow,
As he seemed quite unable to convey, somehow,
The despair and confusion he felt in his mind.
Sherlock spoke to the friar with words firm but kind.

"Your reluctance." said Sherlock, *"is understood well*
For I know there is something distasteful to tell
Which you know you must do and to relay are driven
And you hope that your brothers might yet be forgiven."

"But you are, I can see, a most principled man
Who has come to the city to do what he can
To redress a great wrong and, with courage, redeem
The good name of the friars, their ancient esteem."

*"You've not chosen to stand in a chapel to preach
Hollow words to deaf ears hoping somehow to teach
The self-righteous and pompous how others are wrong
Then sit down and enjoy a repast, great and long."*

*"I deduce you have chosen to face, in your mind,
All the terrors and evils besetting mankind
In a manner befitting your utmost belief -
Your mind is your weapon against all this grief."*

*"In this way, you and I, we are somewhat alike -
With our minds we do battle and step up to strike
At an Evil, deep hidden and hard to dislodge;
It's a challenge to face and one never to dodge."*

*"So, sit back and relax, get your body to rest;
Put your mind to its work and tell me of your quest
In this city of evil, this city of crime -
You have my attention, I grant you my time."*

*"Well, thank you, indeed, Mr Holmes. I am here
To deliver a message, direct but sincere,
To say three of my brothers have all lost their ways
And now follow the Beast in these darkest of days."*

*"Friary Constantine, as it's often called now,
Is a place of reflection and prayer though, somehow,
People think of it being a place of retreat,
A place one may hide and, the world's troubles, cheat."*

*"But it's not, Mr Holmes, it's a place where we come
Face to face with our God trusting there will be some
Way to beg intercession in this Vale of Tears -
It's a place of hard work and we hope that He hears."*

"Whether demons are in us, I truly don't know
But, within all our minds, He seems able to show
Us a glimpse of the Evil which threatens us all -
Perhaps it's a warning for us not to fall."

"But, fall, we all do, although most will arise
To stand tall against Evil in every guise.
And my brothers and I in our tiny commune,
Despite all of our prayers, to its call, aren't immune."

"We can all be perverse, everybody, at times -
From a nasty remark to commission of crimes
Most horrendous as seen on your Whitechapel streets.
We must face up to Evil, not hide 'neath our sheets."

"But we have, on occasion, someone who will hide
A repressed predilection to self-righteous pride.
In this case, it seems three of our number had kept
Such a weakness within them – it grew as we slept."

"Mr Holmes, the three spoke of the action they'd take
Were they given the power from God to remake
This great Empire we live in to one which was fit
For the righteous – the rest would be cast to the Pit."

"Anyone who'd transgress may be judged," said the three,
"And be sent to their fate and have nowhere to flee."
"We'll butcher and damn them," one was heard to say,
"All those fallen women who'd strayed from the Way."

"Mr Holmes," said the friar, *"we told them to cease*
All this talk of such action and all seek release
From that talk, harsh and hateful, they uttered that day
And return to their duties, to reflect and pray."

"For those people, from lives of repression, can't budge.
It's our province to help them, not ever to judge,
For their ways are the ways which great cities impose -
They are ways which not one of them willingly chose."

"The three went on back to their rooms and began,
As it seemed, to behave in a way, to a man,
Which their brothers expected, expending no breath
On divine retribution and dealing out death."

"But those three, Mr Holmes, just on two months ago,
Had decided to leave us – we couldn't say 'No'
For we must each decide for ourselves to remain
Or to leave - from compulsion, our brothers refrain."

"Well, the time came for me to go out and to find
What was good in the world, what assaulted the mind
And what ought to be known to my good brothers, all -
What to pray for the most, what to ask to forestall."

"You might well imagine the shock I received,
And I hoped at the time that I had been deceived,
When I read of the murders in Whitechapel, grim -
The women who'd fallen, each butchered victim."

"The words of my three wayward brothers returned
And assailed my mind as, so fiercely, they burned.
The one far more vocal, I clearly recalled
Uttered words about butchery – we were appalled."

"With no time taken out, not for food nor for sleep,
I sped back to my brothers and told them to keep
On, as never before, with their prayers for the quest
I must now be upon – all our strengths I would test."

"Off to London I started by coach and by train;
I walked mile after mile through wind-driven rain
To connect with a service which left before dawn
And was witness to many an engineer's yawn."

"On arrival at London my heart skipped a beat
For, to come to this city, I felt was a feat
I would never accomplish. I'd never desired
To visit, though now I felt this was required."

"I was lost for a while but I did, on that day,
Ask some helpful policemen to show me the way
To the precincts of your Scotland Yard, which they did -
They were solid, those fellows, not one bit timid."

"I did not want to tell them that I knew the name
Of the killer, the one who would bring us great shame,
For I felt a policeman of junior rank
Would tell me to be off, fearing it was a prank."

"So, with some little effort - it wasn't so hard -
I arrived at the street known as Great Scotland Yard
And proceeded to ask for somebody in charge
Of the case of the Whitechapel killer, at large."

"I was told to 'Be off!' in a manner irate
But I stood and insisted I'd things to relate
On the possible fiend behind all of those acts
So alarming and dreadful – I must tell the facts."

"Mr Holmes, they dismissed me and said I was mad.
I replied I had travelled quite far for I had
Information to share which could well help arrest
This despicable 'Ripper' – I'd things to suggest."

"They said, 'Be off to Bedlam and talk to your friends
In the madhouse, and stay there till this fellow ends
With a kick and a wriggle while fighting the noose.
We do not want the likes of you out on the loose.'."

"I objected again but they said they'd arrest
Me if I kept on being a bothersome pest.
A rather large Sergeant took me by the arm
And said if I stayed I might come to some harm."

"Outside, yet another had something to say -
A young man in plain clothes, but this time in the way
Of some helpful advice, something he'd recommend -
'Seek out Sherlock Holmes up in Baker Street, Friend.'."

"Who it was, I don't know, but I came and I prayed
That the tale of three friars might now be relayed
To somebody who'd listen, somebody who might
Help save even one woman from that dreadful plight."

THE TRIO

Sherlock listened intently – the friar was spent
From his unrested travels – Holmes had to prevent
Him from falling into a great stupor so deep
He'd collapse and, for days, all his data he'd keep.

Holmes needed that data – he wished that his friend
Dr Watson would come back and then recommend,
From his medical knowledge, a draught to revive
The poor friar and keep all his data alive.

"*I can help you, Good Friar, but not for a while.*"
Declared Sherlock Holmes, quite resisting a smile
Of contented excitement on being involved
In the greatest of mysteries yet to solved.

"*My friend and my colleague is now at the Yard
For I have, for some reason, found it very hard
To be given access to the facts of the case -
With luck, very soon I'll be out on the chase.*"

"*He's a medical man – Dr Watson, he's called,
And, together with me, he has found himself stalled
From a great lack of data, in files, locked tight.
I cannot get a look but John Watson just might.*"

"*I suggest, while we wait, you take food and then sleep
Until Watson returns. Take my bed, I will keep
Up a vigil expecting to hear in the street
John Watson, his voice and his galloping feet.*"

"*Take some whiskey, as well, it will settle your mind
And I'd say, in one minute, you'll readily find
That you're falling away to that slumber you need.
When you wake, there'll be work to attend to, indeed.*"

The friar said, "*Thank you, I haven't touched food
For some time, I admit. I've been in such a mood
Of despair and frustration these last many days.
But whiskey – I'm not really used to its ways.*"

"*Strong liquor, Good Friend, this old man has not tasted
For many a year. Many lives have been wasted
When it's taken hold. Do I dare risk a nip?
We swallow a demon with every sip.*"

"Or perhaps it's an angel to bring you some rest."
Replied Holmes, *"And you'll need some to be at your best.*
Everything on this Earth, it should be understood,
Has two sides to it nature - for evil or good."

"So, here, take a sip, and then two and then three,
And the angels within will be able to free
You and settle your mind and then lead you sleep.
The rest they will give you will be long and deep."

"We don't call the drink spirits for nothing, My Friend,
So drink up and then eat is what I recommend."
As directed, the friar took Sherlock's advice
As he prayed that the Devil was not playing dice.

Holmes pointed the way to his bedroom and stated,
"I find excess sleep can be quite over-rated
But do, when exhausted, to slumber descend
So my mind can put all its wild thoughts at an end."

The friar just nodded and went off to bed
Rather hopeful, relaxed and, above all things, fed
And content that, with Sherlock, he now had a chance
To entrap his ex-brothers who'd spoken askance.

Sherlock picked up his pipe for he needed to think.
His supply of tobacco would help the Sleuth shrink
Well away from the mundane and into his mind
Where the hint of a clue he would hope he could find.

It was Watson, however, he needed the most
If he was to have even the hint of a ghost
Of a chance to go chasing the Whitechapel beast
Though his pipe gave him some sort of comfort, at least.

In the meantime, John Watson, ensconced at The Yard
Had been patiently waiting all day on a hard
Quite uncomfortable bench and saw many a sight
Of which some, just a few, almost led to fight.

He observed people coming to make a complaint.
One man, rather portly, proceeded to faint
Dead away – Dr Watson adroitly stepped in
And declared he was filled to the gunwales with gin.

This had gone on and on until Gregson arrived
And explained that, too many times, Watson contrived
To depict the Police as insipid and bland
While Sherlock and he shone out bright in The Strand.

*"Dr Watson, your stories show us as inept
And as useless, completely, although we have kept,
Off the streets, many murderous felons who'd kill
Anyone for a sixpence or, worse still, a thrill."*

*"You've ignored our advice and earned many a Pound
Saying how you and Holmes ran a felon to ground
While Policemen did nothing or got things quite wrong -
What you sang, Dr Watson, is quite an old song."*

*"You make cheap entertainment from poor victims' woes
While you tell everyone we know less than the foes
We go chasing within the constraints of the Law -
When you make us look stupid, it is the last straw."*

*"Do you not understand what it is to be mocked
Everyday by the Public who seem to be shocked
That we cannot find proof for those we might suspect,
That proof which we need but, as yet, can't detect."*

"Do you not think we'd like you on board in this case?
Likewise, Mr Holmes who seems eager to chase
Down Old Jack. Though, to him, it is just a great game
While, to you, it's a story for cash and for fame?"

"Well ... that is ... Mr Gregson ... I'm forced to admit,
Just a little unfair." Watson said just a bit
On the back foot, and seeing Gregson was irate,
"We can find common ground – let us investigate."

"We have orders, explicit, from those upon high
Who'd have our guts for garters to hear you were nigh
And requesting access to the Scotland Yard files."
Said Gregson, *"They want you, from here, many miles."*

"I'll pass onto Lestrade your request but do not
Think that he will be happy being put on the spot
When, the pressure he's under, you cannot conceive.
Here he is – and he's stressed, you'd astutely perceive."

Then, as Lestrade entered, seeing what was in play,
He informed Dr Watson that, early that day,
Yet another horrific offence had occurred
And the wrath of superiors he had incurred.

And the Press and the Public had been on his back
For his lack of success apprehending Old Jack
But he said he'd relent just a little and show
Sherlock Holmes just as much as he needed to know.

Lestrade said they would meet at a time he would say
In the very near future, *"It won't be today*
And perhaps not tomorrow – I have things I must
Now attend to – you will show discretion, I trust."

"Yes, indeed, though I may have to give Holmes a clue
Of what might be on offer to help him subdue
Any urge to go off on his own on a quest."
Watson said to Lestrade, *"I think that would be best."*

"Well, perhaps," said Lestrade, *"just a little to whet*
The man's mad appetite. But I say, don't forget -
Keep that man on a leash, keep him muzzled, at heel,
Or the force of my boot he is likely to feel."

"Now get out of my way, Dr Watson, please go
Before I change my mind and, to you both, say 'No'.
There are things I must do, for my mind is awash
With a vision of evil I may never quash."

With his mission accomplished, Watson hurried back
To the Baker Street digs to tell Holmes that Old Jack
Has been at it again and Lestrade condescends
To let him help a little unless he offends.

Watson opened the outer door, raced up the stairs
To find Sherlock intensely conducting affairs
Of a secretive nature, he chose to deduce,
But was eager for, all his good news, to produce.

"Holmes, My Good Fellow, Lestrade's of a mind
To accept your assistance but you have to find
It within you to dance to The Yard's standard tune -
To refuse, you must know, would be inopportune."

"Well, I shall not refuse." Sherlock said in reply,
"But when you hear my news you will realise why
I'm so often at odds with officialdom's ways
And the great lack of sense it so often displays."

"Your news?" Watson queried, *"Now what could that be?*
Have you gone off and broken your promise to me?
If you've taken a single step out on the street,
You've been reckless and careless and quite indiscreet."

"I meant what I said, Sherlock – tell me no lies.
If you've gone off without me, our partnership dies
For if I cannot trust you for even one day
Then I'll pack my belongings and move straight away."

"I have told you I'll back you, come sunshine or rain,
But in these troubled times I have made it quite plain
That I must have respect and, your word, you must keep.
There are dangers for you, and they're deadly and deep."

Sherlock, taken aback by this verbal assault,
Quickly took the advantage declaring, *"No fault*
In this matter was mine – from this room I've not moved.
This news sought me out - I knew you'd have approved."

"Sought you out! I declare I can't leave you alone
For a moment. You're a man sitting up on a throne
You have made for yourself." Watson quickly replied,
"This high self-esteem is quite undignified."

"Watson!" Holmes countered, *"You know that I hold*
Self-esteem as emotional hum-bug while cold
And dispassionate thinking is my stock-in-trade.
I am rather surprised at this petty tirade."

"In my room, in my bed, is the bringer of news;
A poor habited herald whose weary sinews
Were all stretched near to breaking – he did come to me
When The Yard sent him off. Just how daft can they be?"

"He has news to relate – he has given me hope.
While the forces, official, continue to grope
Their ways forward in darkness pursuing that Blight
Of Whitechapel, we may have stepped into the light."

"Do you mean," broke in Watson, *"this person may hold,*
Fast asleep in your bed, information untold
To Lestrade or his cohorts because someone sent
Him away from The Yard – this is just negligent."

"It is criminal, Watson, a crime of neglect.
It's no wonder the men at The Yard can't detect
Any trace of this Ripper, the one called Old Jack."
Declared Sherlock, agreeing, *"They should get the sack."*

"Not only are they about running 'round blind,
They are stupid as well, and it's not too unkind
To say they should be locked in a cell to protect
Them from him they have failed, so far, to detect."

"Well, who is this herald, exhausted, asleep?
What are all these secrets he's been forced to keep
Till he's found someone willing to listen and heed?"
Watson firmly demand, *"Who is he, indeed?"*

"He's a man of religion, a man of a mind
To face all, as he sees it, the evils which bind
Us forever to action against Evil's ways."
Sherlock answered curtly, *"In short, the man prays."*

"He prays! So do I but, if ever one delves
Into practical matters, those who help themselves
Will more likely be granted assistance, divine."
John Watson insisted, *"This credo is mine."*

"I resist the assertion that prayer on its own
Can persuade the Almighty that we should be shown
The correct way to act – we should know this by now
And, if we need to ask, then we'll never know how."

"Well, this man has prayed long and, also, very hard
But was given short shrift when he went to The Yard
Seeking action from those who have promised to serve."
Ranted Sherlock, *"Perhaps we get what we deserve."*

"Well, it's not us who gets it." John Watson replied,
"The unfortunate women are they who have died
At the hands of a monster who needs to be caught.
I, for one, pray a suitable lesson is taught."

"But enough of this prattle. Just who is this man
Who has travelled to London to do what he can
To assist in the capture of Whitechapel Jack?
There'll be many a cheer when that neck is made crack."

"Well, we first have to catch him before he can strike
Once again in Whitechapel. I fancy you'd like
To be out on his trail." Holmes said, knowing well
That his friend had an urge to send Jack down to Hell.

"Yes, indeed, Mr Holmes," said the friar who'd come
From the bedroom upon overhearing just some
Of what Watson had said about prayer on its own
Being useless in getting Old Jack overthrown.

"I expect," said the friar, *"this man is your friend,*
Dr Watson; a man you took time to commend
For his tact with policemen, an excellent trait
If, on their condescension, you'd ever to wait."

Holmes and Watson stood up just a little surprised
At the words of the friar; they both had surmised
That he'd be rather humble, not worldly at all -
He wasn't that friar Sherlock could recall.

He had gathered his strength and had rested his mind.
He'd regained that composure which would let him find,
Deep within him, the courage to speak and to act -
He found that his nerve was entirely intact.

*"Did we wake you, Good Friar? I hope we did not
With our squabbles so petty – I trust that you got
Enough rest to revive you so that you may tell
Dr Watson and me of the evil you'd quell."*

*"Mrs Hudson will bring us a breakfast, of sorts,
Though it is early evening. The simple comforts
Such as we enjoy here in our Baker Street lair
Keep us both from submitting to abject despair."*

*"So sit down here and join us in what you will find
Will look after the body and nurture the mind.
We'll first hear from Watson who has lots to tell
Then we'll hear what you know of this agent from Hell."*

Sitting down at the table, the three heard a knock
At the door - Mrs Hudson - she said in some shock,
*"Take hot coffee and food - do not let it go cold -
That man's struck again in Whitechapel, I'm told."*

*"In the streets, many mobs are about and adrift,
And a mob won't ask questions, revenge will be swift.
Anyone just suspected will be kicked to death
Or be strung from a lamp post to struggle for breath."*

"I don't know why you sit there – those gifts you possess
Must be able to help the Police, I confess.
Mr Holmes, Dr Watson, get out on the hunt
Or, forever, vacate Baker Street, to be blunt."

"Well said, Mrs Hudson," said Sherlock, alive
For the first time in weeks, *"but we have to contrive*
A new plan with Lestrade, given what we will learn
From this good friar here – for his knowledge, we yearn."

"Just do something before Jack the Ripper can kill
Any more helpless women for some evil thrill
That he gets when they suffer." a rather distraught
Mrs Hudson insisted, *"Mercy, give him naught."*

With that said, Mrs Hudson turned 'round on her heels
And descended the stairs as if she was on wheels.
As the friar and Watson and Holmes ate their meal,
This newly formed Trio had much to reveal.

THE FILES

Watson told of conditions Lestrade had laid down
Saying, if they were broken, then, all over town
Sherlock Holmes would be banned, even possibly kicked
By the boot of Lestrade who disliked being tricked.

"He's a man of his word, and he'll keep it unless
You break yours when he's under such abject duress
From within and without." Watson said to his friend,
"Do not test his resolve or his boot may extend."

"*I confess,*" said the friar, "*to being surprised*
For, to all pull together, I would have surmised
Would have been paramount for the battle ahead
But I find there is nothing but discord, instead."

"*Is it always this way when you're off fighting crime?*
Or is it, in this instance, a singular time
Filled with fear and foreboding for what you may find?
This Lestrade, is he being unduly unkind?"

"*Good Friar,*" said Sherlock, "*this man is a friend*
And a colleague, of sorts, whom I would recommend
As a principled man, but a man who will not
Go outside of the Law to unravel this knot."

"*But it must be unravelled to see if the thread*
Leads to where we'll discover this Agent of Dread
May be hiding, or hidden by others unknown.
Lestrade sticks to the rules but I don't, it's been shown."

"*And this does get between us – and oft times a wedge*
Has been found separating Policemen whose pledge
Holds that Law is inviolable and those who don't
And who, to stick to statutes, cannot or just won't."

"*And that latter is me, Sherlock Holmes, who resists*
Being lawful and nice while the felon persists
With his criminal acts and then rushes to hide
Taking all of the shelter the law books provide."

"*I would rather be sent to a prison than let*
Such a man as this Jack go on killing to get
Any thrill that he may. If I'd not, call me Liar!
If I do break the Law, so be it, My Good Friar."

"Please don't call me Good Friar," he said in return,
*"Friar Geoffrey, I'm known as. Our old names we spurn
And take that of a saint, one we all help select,
A good man of old who has earned our respect."*

*"But, a saint, I am not, just a sinner who copes
With the world in a way which he fervently hopes
Brings improvement to many and warning to those
Who, to follow the Beast and his evil ways, chose."*

*"And, like you, Dr Watson, an oath I have sworn
And, from breaking that pledge, I will never be torn.
But I will not stand by while a handful of laws
Lets a killer go free due to unforeseen flaws."*

*"You have me on your side, though I could never kill
Even though it might mean further blood may well spill
On those streets of Whitechapel – I do pledge my life
And would stand 'tween a victim and Jack's evil knife."*

*"I believe that you would, Friar Geoffrey, and hold
That, of all in this city, you're far more the bold
Man of action than I at first thought you would be."*
Holmes declared, *"After Watson, I'd want you with me."*

*"But we'll wait for Lestrade, I don't want him to think
That I've gone off without him; that surely would sink
Any possible chance that he'd let us assist
In the hunt; otherwise I'd be struck from his list."*

*"Five murders, related - the work of one man
Or one woman, perhaps, who is much stronger than
Any woman I've met, one we cannot discount
Till the facts tell us so when those facts start to mount."*

"And there may have been more murders yet unassigned
To the knife of Old Jack; so we must be resigned
To the prospect of finding more victims who fell
To this object of evil we've sworn we will quell."

"I refuse to be drawn to conjecture based on
The reports in the papers. I'll tell you and John
Those reports of Lestrade, that collection of fact,
I'm impatient to see – I'm impatient to act.

On and on went the day with discussions of crime,
Sherlock happy to kill off the hours of time
Till Lestrade would appear with files he desired
So the game could commence with the data required.

Three men were sprawled out at the Baker Street lair,
Friar Geoffrey asleep in Sherlock's favourite chair,
Dr Watson, a paper pulled over his face,
On the floor Sherlock wanting data to embrace.

Patience could be a virtue, but not at this time
When all that could be heard was the maddening chime
Of the clock in the hallway announcing each hour -
Sherlock knew every chime meant a clue had gone sour.

At last, on the stairs, the familiar sound
Of Lestrade taking two steps with every bound;
He burst into the room where the trio reposed
And presented a folder with data enclosed.

"Wake up!" he insisted, *"You've no time to sleep.*
If they find this file missing, I'm in trouble. deep.
So get up and get thinking – I've one special noose
And it has need of filling with Jack on the loose."

"Lestrade!" Sherlock shouted, *"It is well you have come,
And you've Jack's file with you. We'll also have some
Information to share from the lips of our friend
Friar Geoffrey – to listen, I would recommend."*

Friar Geoffrey had risen from Holmes' favourite chair
Very keen to relate the 'three friars' affair'
To Lestrade of The Yard who was leading the hunt
But to date had received, of all scorn, the full brunt.

"Friar Geoffrey," said Sherlock, *"I'd like you to meet
One of London's best bulldogs whose tread-weary feet
Have been pounding the cobbles by day and by night
Seeking out Jack the Ripper with all of his might."*

*"Meet Inspector Lestrade, he's the best man they've got
Within all Scotland Yard but, as likely as not,
He's been chasing a phantom who's left him no clue
Though he's scoured Whitechapel, to give him his due."*

*"Lestrade, meet Friar Geoffrey, a friend from the north
Who, with tales of trouble, has sallied out forth
To deliver a message to those who would hear
Though his efforts fell on a collective deaf ear."*

"A collective deaf ear? Do you mean Scotland Yard?"
Asked a hard-pressed Lestrade trying ever so hard
Not to pound on the table and yell at the three
With this Whitechapel Jack fellow out roaming free.

"Yes. The man was sent packing while trying to help,"
Holmes replied, *"as if he was some whimpering whelp
Which was being annoying while, truly, the man
Was just being as helpful as anyone can."*

"He has news to relate which may well hold a clue
Which could help to locate this Whitechapel Jack due
For a tightening rope 'round a frightening neck -
Find this fiend so his devilish plans you can wreck."

Lestrade looked at the friar and nodded his head
With disdain on his face, and he said, *"If, instead*
Of me hearing your news, we let Sherlock peruse
Any facts in my file that he thinks he can use."

"When Sherlock is finished, I'll get you to tell
Me your news, and whatever's behind it as well.
You must look in your mind for each pertinent fact
And not let The Yard's conduct toward you detract."

"I can only reflect on the great many pranks
Played upon those deserving of genuine thanks
For the work they have done." Said Lestrade to the friar,
"Eight reports out of ten are the work of a liar."

"Please accept my apologies and my regrets
For that way you were treated. An officer lets
Himself dismiss reports at his peril - each clue
Must be tested so it may be given its due."

"So, Sherlock, they're here, all my Whitechapel files
Holding facts guaranteed to remove any smiles
That you're tempted to have in these terrible times -
They're quite beyond belief, all these terrible crimes."

"We have little to go on but rumours are rife
That this fiend is a demon who uses a knife
Like some devilish artist so he can amuse
Satan deep down in Hades who he can't refuse."

"We've checked suspects aplenty, the list is quite large,
But each one has been cleared so we've no one to charge.
In the streets of Whitechapel, by day, we are mocked
And by night there's the fear of us all being shocked."

"But a fresh pair of eyes such as yours might alert
Us to facts we have missed, facts that we might convert
To a rapid arrest so that Whitechapel Jack -
Is prevented from making a further attack."

Sherlock picked up the file and opened it wide
And saw horror on horror depicted inside
But held back the emotions he started to feel
As his determination had started to steel.

There were five women killed and then grossly defiled
Being butchered, an act leaving Sherlock quite riled
And he said as he bashed his fist down with a bang,
"It would be far too good for this fellow to hang."

"Now, then, steady on, Man," Watson said to his friend,
"You have always told us that you cannot commend
Any fits of emotion when seeking a clue.
The victim deserves that, such things, you subdue."

"And, subdue them, I will," Holmes replied to his friend
"I am not an emotional man and intend
To repress what I feel, which is utter disgust,
But know catching this horror is something I must."

Holmes read on without speaking, his mind all alert
For that small inconsistency which an expert
Highly disciplined mind would pick up as a sign
Which might well show the way to this monster malign.

Three men watched for two hours while pages were turned
And the day turned to night and the oil lamps burned
With their low yellow light till, at last, Sherlock spoke
Saying, *"This is a monster we should not provoke."*

"There is ritual here, but a base sort, I fear,
And the few clues I see shout to me, loud and clear,
That this work is a mixture of dogma and zeal
By a madman who worships some evil ideal."

"But who that man might be, I cannot, I confess,
As yet offer conjecture or hazard a guess
But though, making assumptions, I cannot condone,
I'd say he has resources but works all alone."

"But, missing, are all of those letters received
From anonymous writers for, don't be deceived,
It is certain there'll be valued clues undetected;
I must know if every note was inspected."

"Every note, every word, every scribble was read
And each one was looked into but all leads went dead;
But you're welcome to look," said Lestrade unimpressed
With the way Sherlock had all his hard work addressed.

"But they came in their hundreds, these letters, but all
Were discounted for use for not even one small
Indication of who Jack might be could be found;
It is though this man Jack disappears underground."

"I'll have them sent 'round, every note and each letter.
They've been read every which-way and nobody better
Than those at The Yard could have studied each one -
When it comes to such things we are never outdone."

Sherlock looked at Lestrade and he raised up each hand
Saying, "*There may be none in the whole of this land*
Who can look at a letter and say if a lie
May be written inside, although people still die."

"*The man's still is at large and his name is unknown,*
Though we do call him Jack, and his evil has grown
To the point where he may make a stupid mistake -
We must check every letter then, plans, we must make."

"*But, Lestrade, there is more that you do have to hear*
And it is from this friar who says, loud and clear,
That he might have the answer you've sought all along.
He may well know who Jack is, though he may be wrong."

"*I will ask that you listen – he's come from afar,*
From a place of devotion that's quite insular
Although not as removed from the world as we thought;
To hear what he says, I believe that you ought."

"*I will listen but, first, for those letters I'll send*
So that you may peruse them and then recommend
Any action you feel might result from a clue
We'd not seen." said Lestrade, hoping such would ensue.

Lestrade had Mrs Hudson send Gregson a note
Saying '*bring all the letters which informants wrote*
To me here at Two-twenty-one-B Baker Street
But don't tell anyone who you're going to meet'.

"*I expect it will be quite some time we must wait*
Though that message will go at a fair steady gait
Till it reaches the hand of Gregson at The Yard
For he might be afoot chasing down felons, hard."

"And so, Friar Geoffrey, proceed if you will
And relate what you know. Do you know one who'd kill
In the manner this fiend of Whitechapel has done?
Tell me even if you just suspect anyone."

"You must know I'm not looking for someone to blame
Just to cover my failure, and maybe my shame,
Of not bringing this horror to justice, to date.
If you know, you must tell me, before it's too late."

"Inspector Lestrade," Friar Geoffrey replied,
"I do realise fully you've been occupied
With the task of detecting some sinister ghost
And that you hold that Law has to be uppermost."

"I, too, have respect for those tenets as much
As they protect the innocent; although, as such,
They can also protect those as guilty as sin.
This is no time for Lawyers but Knights Paladin."

THE MONKS

Lestrade looked at the friar and then turned his head
To address Sherlock Holmes, and he said, *"Now I dread*
That another loose cannon's about in this town
Though I cannot deny that I want Jack brought down."

"So tell, Friar Geoffrey, tell me all that you will,
Tell me all that you know of somebody who'd kill
And then butcher these women in some evil rite;
This goes far beyond malice and well beyond spite."

Friar Geoffrey leaned forward and stood Lestrade's gaze
With two eyes in which passion, intense, seemed to blaze
Though he measured his words as he spoke with restraint;
He had facts which he must, with Lestrade, now acquaint.

"May I start with the statement that what I'll now say
May connect in no way with those acts of dismay
Which have fallen on London." the friar declared,
"But for learning they do, I am fully prepared."

"We are, in our Friary, sworn never to speak
In our lives of devotion, but some are so weak
That they just cannot help but say all on their minds.
They are not with us long, these so talkative kinds."

"Of course, there are provisions for speaking when we
Must discuss with each other the things which must be
Given urgent attention, and once every year
One of us goes abroad, both to see and to hear."

"To hear and see what?" the Inspector broke in,
"I'd imagine you'd know of the crime and the sin
In this nation of ours. Isn't that why you seek
Out escape from the world – to be holy and meek?"

"We are neither," the friar responded, *"but try*
To beseech the Good Lord help a world gone awry
And to hold high the sign to the virtuous way.
Our prayers are our weapons - we fight as we pray."

"It had fallen to me to go forth and collect
Any relevant news and also to select
Any items we need for our lives of retreat.
My brothers take news from outside as a treat."

"But imagine the horror when learning of those
Most despicable crimes here in London. I chose
To rush south to tell all of events which occurred
On the Whitechapel streets – down to London I spurred."

"I had tried, as I've said, to report what I knew
To the Forces of Law but, alas, someone threw
Me and my information right out on the street
Though, with somebody helpful, I happened to meet."

"Now I find myself here with two resolute men
And a Police Inspector - yourself - and so when
With such persons who might take my tale as true
I will tell what I know and what I might construe."

"With the greatest regret I am forced to report
That I've news of three men who might well be the sort
To commit such a crime, were their words turned to fact,
Though it's hard to believe they'd commit such an act."

"But, Inspector Lestrade, there were idle monks, three,
In our number who would vocally disagree
With our mode of devotion and used words severe
About taking harsh action – those words bring me here."

"There was one, most of all, saying what should be done
To such women who may have been slain by the one
Who they call Jack the Ripper. Inspector, please note
He said 'Butcher and damn them' – exact words I quote."

"He said what?" yelled Lestrade as he jumped to his feet,
"This indeed is a man I'd be anxious to meet
And demand he explain why he felt he might say
Anyone in this land should be treated that way."

54

"Tell me more, tell me all." the Inspector insisted,
"Leave out nothing and tell if this fellow persisted
In saying these things over time or if he
Just exploded one day letting foolish words free."

"He voiced, more than once, his invective so vile
Though he would hold his overused tongue for a while,
Which of course is what is, of our brothers, expected
Though some recommended that he be ejected."

"He had passion within him; the man had the gift
Of exceptional vigour which we thought might lift
Up his mind to have thoughts of a generous kind
But it seems that he let evil loose in his mind."

"His two friends, I would say, had been both led astray
And succumbed to temptation and so took the way
Which is easy to follow but hard to retrace
When, the evil it leads to, such types have to face."

"It is hard to say 'No' to the way of the Beast
For that way looks so easy though even the least
Little step one might take one finds hard to take back
For it's slippery and steep on that dark downward track."

"It's much better, by far, if we stick to the trail
Put there for us to follow though it may entail
Us to clamber our ways over rough rocky ground
For the way of the righteous, though trying, is sound."

"And it's many've been tempted, and found to great cost,
That they have, to the darkness, forever been lost
Having veered from that path to one offering ease
Then delivering naught but the Beast's evil tease."

"*Friar Geoffrey,*" Lestrade interrupted to say,
"*I appreciate well that we all often stray*
From the paths we should follow, but show me the track
I must follow to collar old Whitechapel Jack."

"*Ah, yes. Please forgive me.*" the Friar replied,
"*That my tongue has been loosened cannot be denied*
But, if you can bear with me, I think I might show
You the man and the monster that you need to know."

"*Do go on,*" said Lestrade, "*But my time's not my own*
And the ire of the Whitechapel people has grown
To the point where they'll string me up high with a rope
If I cannot deliver just one ray of hope."

"*I expect that soon, Gregson my colleague, will come*
With those letters I sent for and so perhaps some
Little clue we have missed Sherlock Holmes will detect
Though it will lead to nothing I'm led to expect."

"*So if you, Friar Geoffrey, can speed up your tale,*
We might then breathe new life to enquiries gone stale.
I would like to hear more of this friar gone bad
So, to get to that point, very soon, I'd be glad."

"*Ah, yes,*" said the friar, "*that point, I'm approaching.*
It is quite a delicate subject I'm broaching
For it is a great confidence which I betray
But my options are naught in this case, I would say."

"*The two friars who'd follow the lead of the one*
Who said words about butchery, often had done
Only what they had felt would get praise from that other,
Our ever so vocal, unwise errant brother."

"That friar was called, it should be understood,
Friar Jacques after one who was pious and good.
This was not his real name but one which he assumed
When he came to live with us, with passion, consumed."

"Those two which had followed assumed, each, a name
Of a good man of old on the day each became
Taken into our number – they each took an oath
They would walk the straight path and, to falter, be loath."

"We are, none of us, perfect; none totally good.
We are formed out of flesh, that is well understood,
And the flesh can be weak, therefore spirit must fight
All the forces which steer us away from the light."

"Friars Andrew and George, as the names might suggest,
Took their saints' names for Scotland and England in zest
By these two weaker men although neither could claim
To live up to their namesakes – too high was their aim."

"They did not give their names – it was never required
To disclose anything any man had desired
To leave outside our doors, but I had heard some say
That the Scot was called Rufus; the Englishman, Ray."

"More than that I can't tell you about these two men
Only they behaved well up until the time when
Friar Jacques started spreading his gospel of hate
And I fear, for our brothers, we acted too late."

"Brother this, Friar that." said Lestrade, breaking in.
"Are the titles the same or perhaps just akin
To each other. I sometimes have felt quite confused
When one term or the other is casually used."

"Brother's English, Friar's Latin." the friar replied,
"And they both mean the same but with Brother applied
We're expressing a friendship we all think is normal -
With Friar we're, as often as not, being formal."

"We may likewise say friar while we'll also use
The term monk for the person – such terms we abuse
Just a little through usage - they interchange well.
Detective, Inspector – the same, some would tell."

Lestrade nodded a *'thank you'* and Sherlock concurred
While Watson, amused, had been gingerly spurred
To break into a smile he tried to contain
While from laughing out loudly, he had to refrain.

Friar Geoffrey continued, in his humble way,
In describing the brothers who'd been led astray
When the sound of Police boots ascending the stairs
Caused the group, all as one, to leap up from its chairs.

It was Gregson with letters, in bundles all bound,
Saying, *"These are the letters, all that I had found*
In the files marked 'Inspected' and several which came
In the mail this morning – some types have no shame."

"They would keep us away from our fight against Jack
And I would like to say, if I could answer back,
What I'd do to a person who might get a thrill
By pretending to know when and where Jack will kill."

"They can write out their letters and post them away
So they must understand they will lead us astray
And give Jack opportunity to commit more
Of those acts which all London is right to deplore."

"I would lock them away in a dungeon so deep
That they'd never be heard from – we'd not hear a peep
Or receive one more letter." the Inspector cried,
"I'd break all their fingers if they even tried."

"Well, Gregson," Holmes said, *"you are not one to beat*
'Round the bush on such matters but, meanwhile, a treat
Was about to come forth from the lips of our friend,
Friar Geoffrey - to wait is what I'd recommend."

Friar Geoffrey continued, Gregson standing mute
With his bundles of letters which would constitute,
Within his mind at least, of their time, a great waste;
But he was asked to bring them along in great haste.

Gregson looked at the friar who looked back in turn
And it seems Gregson's eyes both had started to burn.
At the friar he nodded and then shook his head
Pointing straight at Lestrade with a look of some dread.

It was he, unbeknown to the rest, who had sent
Friar Geoffrey to Holmes with a definite scent
Of someone who might be or might show them the track
To the scourge of all London, that Whitechapel Jack.

The friar took the message and he understood
That the junior Inspector's intentions were good
But he didn't want any Policeman to know
That he would, such a clue, onto Sherlock Holmes, throw.

Then the friar, in brief, for Gregson's benefit,
Explained what he had missed till he got to the bit
About butchery mentioned by one of the three,
The one who, from vision, had now broken free.

"As 'Butcher and damn them' were spoken by him
And directed at women who'd fallen victim
To the evils of London, I fear he's the one
That you're all calling Jack and he must be undone."

"Friar Jacques was a loner at first but he drew
In these men, weak in spirit, and soon we all knew
We should keep them apart, but the man was so sly
That he led them astray as the long months went by."

"The name which he had before taking his vow
Was a name of some stature which he had, somehow
And some time in his life, brought into disrepute.
His need to atone seemed sincere and acute."

"It was Lord Basilthwaite, christened Rupert, who came
To our group to renounce and forget his old name.
None but I and one other and, naturally he,
Knew the name he'd forsaken – tight-lipped we must be."

"Friar Jacques he became; he showed merit at first
But, for wayward behaviour, developed a thirst.
Inspectors, we'd not heard of any attack
In Whitechapel when we dubbed the man Brother Jack."

"Brother Jack!" Holmes exploded, *"It would be, I'd say,*
A coincidence great; so we four here this day
Must agree not to mention this man's assumed name.
The response from the Press we could not hope to tame."

Watson jumped to his feet to consult the great book
On the peerage of Britain – no great time it took
To locate in its pages that family name -
Would the entry list greatness and honour, or shame?

In those long lists of Peers, Watson found only one
Mention of this old family, one brought quite undone
Sometime deep in the past as, from fate or poor luck,
From prominence, it had withdrawn or been struck.

THE LETTERS

Lestrade thanked Friar Geoffrey for what he had told
And he turned 'round to Gregson and gave him a cold
Look of some disapproval, though knowing full well
He'd have done the same thing, if the truth he must tell.

He had seen what had passed, when the letters appeared,
'Tween the Friar and Gregson – he often had feared
That the junior Inspector had oftentimes sought
The advice of the Sleuth so much more than he ought.

But, now knowing the reason, Lestrade was tight-lipped
For he too, on occasion, was known to have slipped
From the law-restrained precincts of Great Scotland Yard
To the Baker Street lair if a case proved too hard.

Gregson took the occasion to speak up before
Lestrade had any chance to display any more
Than a look of disdain - he said, "*Sir, as required,
I've brought you the letters you said you required.*"

"*And it's not before time.*" Lestrade said with a huff
Although all there could see it was just the man's bluff
Showing who was in charge even though he would draw
On the skill of someone who worked beyond the Law.

"Well, that is a large pile." Watson said in alarm
At the letters Gregson carried under his arm.
Gregson said in reply, *"Many hundreds, I'd say.*
So many, and more coming in every day."

"And each one must be read for what it might contain
Till the eyes of policemen go red with the strain
Brought about by deciphering wording so bad
It would send any teacher of English quite mad."

"But we must check each one, not dismiss any just
For its contents, ridiculous. Each and all must
Be looked into for clues although most will be found
To be works of great mischief by minds quite unsound."

"It must take you forever to check every one."
Watson said, *"I'm appalled if such mischief is done*
By some people who must be completely deranged.
They'd object if their innards became rearranged."

"Quite so, Dr Watson. Though, complain, I would not.
It would be just desserts that such stupid types got
If The Ripper found them on a dark London street."
Said Lestrade in reply, *"What an end they would meet."*

"While they're feeling the blade cutting into their flesh,
Let them put pen to paper and send us a fresh
Letter saying how they know where Jack can be found.
I would drop what I'm doing and come right around."

"Well, that's what I might do only if fate were fair,
But the way of it is that I tear out my hair
Every time that some ignorant fool pens a note -
Within may be a clue though the chance is remote."

"So, Sherlock, please use all those powers you keep
In that strange minds of yours – anything hidden deep
In those letters received you are able to find
Will prove you have the vision while we are all blind."

Holmes took from the Inspector the letters he'd brought
Telling all in the room that, for some time, he ought
To be left in the room all alone to peruse
What had, up to that point, only served to confuse.

"I need space, I need quiet. Please, all, go away.
All of you know my methods – I'll be led astray
From the task which I now undertake if I hear
Anyone drawing breath, anyone standing near."

"Give me room; move those chairs and that table as well.
On this floor I will see what these letters can tell
Of that fiend of our streets, of our Whitechapel Jack.
Let me spread out these words – I have clues to attack."

Watson said to the rest, *"We should all take our leave*
For when Sherlock gets going he's likely to heave
Anything in his way to the side or away.
He becomes quite obsessive, I'm compelled to say."

So, all did as suggested and left Holmes alone;
The detectives returned to The Yard with a tone
To their voices more hopeful than heard for some time -
For Sherlock, they knew, was a crime-solver prime.

With the friar, however, Watson didn't know
What to do, how to act, what emotion to show
With this man of the cloth quite unversed in the ways
Of the city he loved, though now deep in dismay.

It was too late for walking and seeing the sights
And one ambled in peril below feeble lights.
He considered the man wouldn't visit a pub
And so Watson decided it must be his club.

"If you wish, Friar Geoffrey, we might take a walk
To a place I frequent where we might sit and talk
And perhaps take a supper while Sherlock attacks
All those letters to see if one's Whitechapel Jack's."

"It's my club into which I must often retreat
Anytime my friend Sherlock feels forced to entreat
That, our rooms which we share for a while, I vacate,
So on problems quite weighty he can concentrate."

"Yes, of course," said the friar by way of reply,
"Mr Holmes seems a fellow quite hard to defy
Once he's hard on the scent of a quarry at large.
He seems like a warrior set for the charge."

"He would make a good friar should he ever opt
For the life of reflection and prayer we adopt
Though I do really think that our ways would seem tame
To a man such as he, though our aims are the same."

"Well I fear," countered Watson, *"if that came to pass,*
Sherlock Holmes in his silent moods might well outclass
Any ten of your brothers; but if he should speak
All attempts made to gag him would prove rather weak."

"He has gifts which he uses," the friar broke in,
"And he does seem to use them against all the sin
In this city, this country, and lands far beyond,
Though I feels it's excitement of which he is fond."

"That it is," agreed Watson, *"he lives for the thrill*
Of the chase, the adventure – he must have his fill
Of the danger around him while using his wits.
The man is a hunter; the man never quits."

"But his heart is a good one and, thank God, I do,
For, if he were to follow the dark ways, then who
Here among us could stop him – his mind is a tower
Of strength which exudes a remarkable power."

"Well now, here, for an hour or two, perhaps three,
We may stop while that brain is allowed to run free
Unencumbered by spurious thoughts generated
By types such as us – let the man stay fixated."

Up the steps went the Doctor, the Friar in tow,
To his favourite club; meanwhile Sherlock could throw
Himself into the problem of letters diverse
From, perhaps, Jack the Ripper, that horror perverse.

Sherlock Holmes, when in harness, always needed space
For his unhindered mind to continue apace.
It must not be distracted by people who'd peer
Over shoulders, ask questions – at such types he'd sneer.

He would also need space to spread letters around
On the floor, unimpeded; the man must surround
Himself with all the data he sensed held a clue -
Several lines of suspicion, he knew, would be due.

He'd reject all of those he considered to be
Of a mischievous nature, although even he
Would be careful when so many lives were at stake -
He'd take what time he'd need for the next victim's sake.

But time was now pressing – permission to read
All the letters came after Watson went to plead
That the keen eyes of Sherlock be given a chance
While official decrees would refuse him a glance.

Sherlock knew that the prospects of finding a clue
In those masses of letters were poor, but a true
And determined detective must never neglect
Any chance, any snippet of truth, to detect.

He read through every letter at speed but discarded
The bulk as a mischief - his great mind bombarded
With facts, true and false, giving each one its due
Till he felt he detected the hint of a clue.

He placed several aside for he sensed that a game
Was in play in Whitechapel – just one letter came
In a hundred that gave even one tiny hint
Of the evil prevailing, the merest imprint.

No pattern emerged for some time but Sherlock
Had a mind which could filter the facts and then lock
Onto one single feature within the great mass
Of some ten thousand others, that jumbled morass.

He saw one, then another, whose words seemed to link
And this caused Sherlock Holmes to consider and think
On the message within should those links form a chain;
The great game was afoot – Sherlock could not refrain.

Most were drivel, he knew, but a dozen he chose
From the hundreds presented; and when Sherlock rose
With that handful of letters, the faint call he sensed
Of the hunt-master's bugle – the Sleuth's muscles tensed.

The letters he held in his hand seemed to say,
So much more than the rest he had thrown away,
And from only one hand it would seem each one came,
The tones were alike and the theme was the same.

He knew Gregson would fume at the way he had scattered
Each unwanted letter like it hadn't mattered
That it had been sorted and bundled with care.
Luckily, each was labelled, its date to declare.

The evidence gathered by Scotland Yard must
All be well documented - Lestrade put his trust
To keep order, in Holmes, to higher degree -
If a crime can't be proven, the felon goes free.

Sherlock's world, though, was messy, the man was a slob
Of the highest of orders when hot on the job
Seeking clues about why all these women were killed -
The Yard's expectations might not be fulfilled.

From an orderly mass to a wide-scattered mess
Sherlock rendered the files, though feeling success
Would be all he'd require, in his estimation,
And he had, in his hand, ample justification.

There were twelve letters chosen by Holmes on that night
And each one held a link in a chain, or it might
If the theme of the message each page had displayed
Proved a clue which might have Jack the Ripper betrayed.

Some groupings of letters came from the same hand
But only one grouping, Holmes found, would demand
Further scrutiny due to the challenge, presumed,
Offered up the writer – Sherlock was consumed.

He stood up, looked around – it came as a surprise
That he'd been left alone which he thought was unwise
Even though he could be an impossible wretch
When out chasing a clue with his mind at full stretch.

"Mrs Hudson." he barked, but received no reply
For the lady retired and bid all *"Goodbye"*
As the others crept off, leaving Holmes to his quest.
They did not, Sherlock's ego or ire, want to test.

Sherlock Holmes held some clues but had no one to tell
Of what he had uncovered – he wanted to yell
To Lestrade that he'd found what The Yard couldn't see
But, alas, was alone, all forsaken by three.

By date of receipt he set out letters, twelve,
And examined the game into which he must delve.
Sherlock said to himself, *"I had not, I confess,
Ever thought of this Whitechapel Jack playing chess."*

*"But here falls the first pawn, a poor woman who'd not
Ever hurt anyone in her life but who got,
For the life forced upon her, a death undeserved.
The first to make all over London unnerved."*

*"She finds mention in code, if I am not deceived,
But the code is so simple it might be received
As a taunt by a mind dissolute and depraved
Yet aware that restraint could have had her life saved."*

*"It's deliberate cruelty if that is the case.
Just the vile expression of someone quite base
Who must see others suffer for what is perceived
As a wrong done somehow to one quite self-deceived."*

"This person's not mad but has opted to follow
The path of that one whose false promise is hollow;
He knows what he does and he knows it is wrong
But he likes how it feels for it makes him feel strong."

"That's his weakness, however, and one we must make
Work against him to beat him and then he can take
Thirteen steps to the scaffold – to Hell we'll send back
This expression of Evil, this Whitechapel Jack."

Through Sherlock, unexpected emotion ran wild
And he felt, for a moment, the thrill which a child
Undergoes when the time for a birthday comes due -
As a gift, he'd received what he knew was a clue.

He should tidy the clutter he'd made, well he knew,
But the way of the Sleuth was to focus his view
Onto what he had gathered, not clean up the mess
Left behind in his wake – all such thoughts he'd repress.

He would also repress all emotion for he,
As the ultimate Sleuth on a case, had to be
Sharply focussed on finding more clues from Old Jack
And would not waste a minute on putting things back.

Just as midnight was striking, Watson closed the door
Of Two-twenty-one-B treading, softly, the floor
Hoping not to disturb Mrs Hudson's repose;
With the friar behind him, upstairs the man rose.

The door to their rooms, Watson opened with care,
For to interrupt Holmes was a thing he'd not dare.
When he saw Sherlock staring and hard at his task
He said, *"Holmes, have you found anything, may I ask?"*

THE CHESSMEN

Sherlock Holmes didn't stir as his two friends returned.
He was reading intently the words which had burned
They ways into his mind and would not settle down.
Sherlock Holmes was on fire though his face wore a frown.

From one note to another the Sleuth switched his gaze
As he tried to find order within such a maze
But, abruptly, he stopped when he heard the floor creak -
He looked up and he finally took time out to speak.

"Watson, Friar Geoffrey, you've come none too soon.
I've detected a pattern which might be a boon
To our investigations, though I must confess
That I didn't suspect Jack the Ripper played chess."

"Played chess? What the Devil ... what is that you say?"
Dr Watson enquired, *"Well, chess, he might play*
But what has that to do with these letters afloat
On our floor? You know Gregson will go for your throat."

"This scatter of letters, you know, is the thing
To incense Scotland Yard and would cause it to bring
Down the Damocles' Sword hanging over your head.
Could you not have been tidy, a little, instead?"

"Friar Geoffrey, if more of your time, I may plead,
Could you help with these letters so Sherlock may read
All the clues he desires? We must rebuild each stack
For Lestrade on the warpath is worse than Old Jack."

Friar Geoffrey replied, *"Well, of course, tell me how.*
If they're marked in date order, that's sure to allow
Us to sort all those letters in no time at all.
Mr Holmes seems obsessive when he's heard the call."

"Obsessive." said Watson, *"A gross understatement.*
Sherlock Holmes doesn't see any need for abatement
Or reduction of anything feeding his brain.
When the man's on a case he's an absolute pain."

"But a pain with a purpose." Friar Geoffrey declared
As both he and Watson knelt down and prepared
To sort letters by date to avoid Lestrade's ire.
"Mr Holmes may have found what we all would desire."

"Gentlemen," broke in Sherlock, their banter ignoring,
"I have been hard at work while you both were exploring
The soft cushioned chairs set around Watson's club
While these clues have been circling my cranial hub."

"Don't complain about mess when I'm digging for gold
And have found shiny nuggets entrenched in a cold
And resistant matrix." to his friends said Sherlock,
"I am bound to make rubble when hammering rock."

"Yes, I know of your rubble, the stuff that you strew
All about our poor diggings, but surely a few
Little moments of tidying up wouldn't hurt."
Was all the good Doctor could think of to blurt.

"But how did you know we had been at my club?"
Watson asked of his friend's circled cranial hub.
"We might well have visited 'most anyone.
Any medical colleague of mine would have done."

"Elementary, My Friend. It's the cigar you smoked.
Its aroma that lingers in no time invoked
A response in my brain, for your club stocks the best
Trichinopoly brand. So, my case, I now rest."

71

"But if you need more, on you coat I perceive
Ash from such a cigar as you always receive
When you sit in those chairs and you're forced to recline
Horizontally, almost, compressing your spine."

"All your friends that I know prefer smoking a pipe
And you left me a clue when you failed to wipe
Off that tell-tale ash, so specific, sublime -
I'll prepare a short monograph when I get time."

"Friar Geoffrey," said Watson, *"see what I endure.*
For Sherlock's perception there isn't a cure.
He knows where I've been, who I've seen, what I've done
Anytime, anywhere, anything, anyone."

"I see a great gift and I understand why
I was sent to your friend forced to stand idly by
While a fiend was at large." Friar Geoffrey declared,
"And if I was this Jack, I'd prepare to get scared."

The friar sat back on his haunches to hear
The Great Sleuth's call to arms, loud and ever so clear.
"Well said, Friar Geoffrey. The crux you have found.
Now it's time to get running this villain to ground."

"I believe he has left us twelve viable clues;
Clues which tell me that Jack is a man who pursues
Infamy in a way which would see gratified
The delusions his devilish ego supplied."

"The man has education, his knowledge of chess
Would suggest that, though evil, he has none-the-less
Had spare time to indulge in such games of the mind.
He might crave recognition, he may be that kind."

"And his bestial side, his depravity may,
Detailed medical knowledge, in some way betray
For his victims show signs of a surgical hand
And of eyes used to gore but a heart cold and bland."

"He perhaps is like Watson in some of his traits
But, unlike our good Doctor for whom Heaven waits
And who's tended the wounds of a battlefield's crop,
This man full of evil does not want to stop."

"His letters I hold show for each evil act
He's sent one in advance and one after the fact
Making six acts in all, though he's credited five;
Perhaps one unknown victim may still be alive."

"But the savagery shown has increased with each crime
So this victim would be of the earliest time.
We must plough through the records for such an event -
If we're lucky, this victim might prove Heaven-sent."

"This writer of letters first speaks of a pawn
Who must be sacrificed, and the reader is drawn
To believe this is simply an opening move
In a game with so many chessmen to remove."

"The second suggests that this pawn has been killed
And goes on to describe how so much blood was spilled
And how much more will flow till the city runs red
As the evil that walks it is thoroughly bled."

John Watson spoke up while the friar stayed mute
And he asked if the files from The Yard could refute
Or confirm such a claim, and the Great Sleuth replied,
"Two came on the day that first victim died."

"Those files only start after Whitechapel Jack
Had despatched his first victim in his first attack
But that first letter sent is included with those
For the five women victims we know that he chose."

"So, perhaps the man failed on attempting his first
Knife attack on a victim but still had a thirst
To deliver more horror and so struck once more
This time leaving a body enveloped in gore."

"Both attacks must have been on the very same day
For two letters were posted together, I'd say,
Sometime after the first which warned of an attack -
One to gloat, one to warn of new work from Old Jack."

"If no body was found then the victim might live
And might have information quite vital to give.
We must find out where-ever that victim resides -
Somewhere in this city, that first victim hides."

"She may be with family or with, perhaps, friends
But the news of more victims perhaps recommends
To herself and her helpers that she ought not tell
The Police of her brush with this agent of Hell."

"She may not be hurt badly for, if she had been,
It would be necessary for her to be seen
By a hospital doctor and Jack would soon hear
That his work was unfinished and he'd soon appear."

"We must seek out Lestrade and insist that he seek
Out a woman who needed attention that week
After Jack started killing and mailing his taunts
And his warnings of upcoming Whitechapel jaunts."

"We must seek out a man with pretentions to fame
But who seeks out revenge in his devilish game;
He has culture to boast, or did have at one time;
He asserts false morality with every crime."

"He must lurk in the shadows, he can't stand the light
For if he is identified then he just might
Be shown up for the pretence such fellows exude.
He fears, I believe, his own ineptitude."

"That describes Friar Jacques," Friar Geoffrey suggested,
"The man refused meekness and always contested
The ways of our Friary, refusing to serve -
He demanded esteem which he didn't deserve."

"He could well have played chess – he was certainly born
To a higher estate than myself and I've sworn
That his family was noble, in some minor way,
And he simply refused to throw all that away."

"But, for medical knowledge, there's nothing I know;
No light on that subject I'm able to throw;
But the man was intelligent, that I can say,
Though his arrogant manner would get in his way."

"You said six pairs of letters, twelve letters in all,
Five definite victims and one we might call
A fortuitous error if, find her, we can."
John Watson said calmly, *"Not much of a plan."*

"It's a start," declared Sherlock, *"but I do agree*
That the plan we prepare is a plan which we three
In this room must devise before Scotland Yard finds
What is on and declares that we're out of our minds."

"*Lestrade wants our help, his superiors don't;*
Gregson is on side but we know that he won't
Go directly against any orders received -
We may be on our own - of that, don't be deceived."

"*Well, before we make plans,*" Dr Watson broke in,
"*You must know that our knowledge is really quite thin.*
Tell us more of those letters you hold in your hand,
Of the clues that you seem to have at your command."

"*The first two pairs of letters you said had referred*
To one victim, unknown, who survived when Jack erred
And another who died at the scene of the crime.
Tell us of the next four lest we run out of time."

"*Yes, I will,*" replied Sherlock, "*the threats are quite clear*
And will not be the last we'll receive, I do fear.
The third threat says a pawn will go down to a knight
And will die in the street with no hint of a fight."

"*Gentlemen – 'to a knight' - now his tone is displaying*
His own self-delusions. Or is he relaying
The actual title he feels he deserves,
Or is it to unsettle more fragile nerves?"

"*In the fourth pair of letters, the killer writes more*
Of the same with the mention of more deaths in store
For this city he says is unworthy and must
Suffer death at the hands of one noble and just."

"*The man seems mad to me.*" said John Watson, "*I can't*
See how any sane person could act so. I shan't
Sleep a wink till we run this mad fellow to ground
And he finds that, a place on the gallows, he's found."

"Madness," countered Sherlock, *"would surely exclude*
Any talk of the gallows – the man would elude
What he richly deserves – he is sane, I declare,
And, of what he is doing, is fully aware."

"Take victim number four, foully murdered was she
But the warning received was that there was to be,
By a bishop, a move on a pawn in a square
And the work of his knights would give London a scare."

"Pawns, bishops and knights and a darkened square say
That the writer has sent us a challenge to play
In a scholarly game just to prove that he's clever,
But to rise to that bait is a thing we'll do, never."

"But, to catch him, we may find that chess has a use
For the man is obsessed and is clearly obtuse
For he thinks that he is a superior kind
And possesses, he thinks, a superior mind."

"We shall use that against him, but not play his game
And he'll find that the forces against him aren't tame
When we start dealing cards from keenly marked deck.
He will soon feel the noose 'round his arrogant neck."

"The game we shall play from now on will be poker -
He'll not be a knight but a laughable joker.
Playing chess, he will find, is a fight to the death
And he'll pay with his life, with his terminal breath."

"But what of the fifth?" Watson asked knowing well
That the tale would be truly horrific to tell.
"She had died, so they say, from a frenzied attack
Then was butchered in earnest by Whitechapel Jack."

"Yes. I've seen police pictures." Holmes had to admit,
"And I'd grant to the fellow not one little bit
Of compassion or mercy, nor rush to his aid
If he, too, met that fate – I'd stand back, I'm afraid."

"There had been a sixth letter and also its pair -
One to warn, one gloat on the horrid affair
And I fear there'll be more, even worse, that may come
It may not just be Jack but a deadly threesome."

"A bishop, two knights make a total of three
And it wouldn't take much to get me to agree
These are three errant friars, one evil, two weak -
Friar Geoffrey, if you disagree you should speak."

"Sadly, Mr Holmes, I am forced to concur
With your words, even though it's a horrible slur
On our order, my brothers – with hindsight I'd say
That I should have delved more on that admission day."

"How could anyone know? Who could ever believe
That this man of the cloth could cause London to grieve
Over murders so foul by a man so depraved."
Dr Watson responded, *"Great evil he craved."*

"To Lestrade we'll relate what we've learned here tonight
And convince him to let me get into this fight.
For, while Scotland Yard dithers, this man plans to kill
Not for God, not for Satan, but just for the thrill."

Sherlock despatched a message explaining that he
Had come up with a plan in which Jack might well be
Brought to book and to justice – *"No one has to know*
Sherlock Holmes is involved – it will still be your show."

Sherlock knew that he must, in this instance, be kept
In the shadows – a place he found hard to accept.
He would don his disguises, go forth and cavort
With the criminal class but, to Lestrade, report.

A campaign of his own Sherlock Holmes must not wage;
He declared, Jack the Ripper, he would not engage.
One more thing to Lestrade Sherlock Holmes had to say,
"If one note mentions chess, let me know right away."

THE VICTIM

Five victims were dead but one might be alive
And the trio, with help from Lestrade, must contrive
Any way they may contact victim number one
And then how they may bring Jack the Ripper undone.

This was not to be easy, they thought, but they would,
With the contacts of Watson, find out where one could
Seek out medical help for the knife wounds inflicted
That very first night as the letter predicted.

"No mention was made," pondered Holmes, *"of a knight,*
Nor of two with a bishop – I think this fact might
Point to some change of plan as The Ripper found he
Was not quite the grand killer he thought he would be."

"For he may have met with some resistance that first
Night he chose to spill blood for his devilish thirst.
He may then have discovered, to hold victims still,
He would need extra hands to deliver a kill."

"He goes forth under cover of dark seeking those
Who are very much weaker than he, but he chose
Someone very determined to preserve her life
On that very first time that he struck with his knife."

"But she would be quite nervous to make a report
To Police or the Press who had made so much sport
On the first fatal victim of Whitechapel Jack -
She'd be scared of him following up his attack."

"So our efforts to find her must be quite discreet
For she's bound to be wary of big Police feet
Charging in her front door asking questions galore -
She must know that she's safe and will suffer no more."

"Friar Geoffrey, I'll ask you to stay here till we,
That is Watson and I, go about to find she
Who I'm sure is in hiding, injured but alive -
She may help us stop Jack killing more than those five."

"Are we sure she was hurt?" Watson asked of his friend,
"She, perhaps, may have gotten away in the end
With no wound to her person, just fearful and shocked,
And now hides behind doors firmly bolted and locked."

"A distinct possibility," Sherlock replied,
"Though the tone of the letter received had implied
She was stabbed and her body was left on the ground
Though we know such a victim had never been found."

"Either way, we must help her and put her at ease
And, her obvious fear, we must try to appease
So she may well remember, if we are discreet,
Who attacked her and left her to die in the street."

"Yes, Holmes," broke in Watson, *"discreet we must be*
For, if found in Whitechapel, a pair such as we
Would arouse the suspicion of types who don't trust
Anyone asking questions – be careful, we must."

"We'd stand out like sore thumbs and be lied to, at best,
For such questions would lead to a deal of unrest
And a hostile mob would assemble forthwith
To attack those who threaten their kin or their kith."

"They're a people apart in Whitechapel's back streets
And a beating, most savage, is something which greets
Anyone who attempts an incursion to find
Someone hiding within them, someone of their kind."

Sherlock Holmes gave John Watson a look of disdain
In which one could detect both derision and pain
On receiving a lecture on how matters stand
In this city he knew like the back of his hand.

"You don't think, do you Watson, I'd enter that place
Where Police would arrest me if even a trace
Of a rumour went forth that, abroad, I had been -
On those streets of Whitechapel, I will not be seen."

"But I have, as you know, ventured out in disguise
For I have the ability to improvise
And become a new person, a vicar perhaps,
And be quite overlooked by those Whitechapel chaps."

"Those fellows aren't saints but they do have a code
Which permits men of God to invade their abode
Just as long as God's men don't point fingers and judge
For, from lives rough and ready, they will never budge."

"Or, perhaps, as a loafer, I might find a chair
In a tavern and settle in abject despair,
It would seem to the patrons, and listen for clues
As the tongues start to wag and the bragging ensues."

"Or you might, if your colleagues are trustworthy sorts,
Ask if any have had or have heard of reports
Of a woman so injured and seeking out aid
Or of one just attacked and who's simply afraid."

While the friar remained doing what he did best,
Watson set off to question his colleagues - a quest
Which he knew would be hard for they did, as did he,
Remain silent about any patients they'd see.

But he'd try to get 'round this by saying he'd not
Divulge names or reveal what locations he got.
He'd insist that his quest was a two-fold attack:
Keep the victim quite safe and catch Whitechapel Jack.

He'd ask them to keep mum on his quest lest they might
Alert Whitechapel - Jack Holmes elected to fight
Such an evil as his with his powers so keen
But, essential, it was that his part stay unseen.

Holmes, himself, would go forth in disguises he knew
Had worked well in the past – he was keen to renew
Those acquaintances made in personas diverse -
With the best and the worst in the land he'd converse.

Down to Spitalfields, then on to Whitechapel's pubs,
Sherlock, dressed as a loafer, accepted the snubs
He received from the publicans wanting the space
For their hard-drinking patrons that he might displace.

He would buy one more drink and then shuffle around
To a dark dingy corner to hear every sound,
Every word, that was uttered by tongues wagging hard,
Ever hopeful for clues - ever ready - on guard.

There was less talk of victims than that of who might
Be behind all the killings and whether, tonight,
Jack the Ripper would strike with his knife sharp and keen
And of how such a killer had never been seen.

There was talk of Jack being a phantom who could,
When he wanted, take on any shape that he would;
All the night he would prowl then would vanish before
Big Ben heralded dawn, leaving panic and gore.

Some insisted The Ripper was medically trained
And, though quite without mercy, was oddly constrained
To the region 'round Spitalfield's ancient enclaves -
The old Hospital Fields full of uncounted graves.

It was said that he rose every night from his tomb
Where he hid from the light in that shadowy womb
To be reborn and roam by the feeble moonlight
Taking victims to his and the Devil's delight.

Others countered by saying Jack could be a toff
But disgraced and, from home and his family, sent off
For some evil he did which no one could forgive -
For this, he'd decided that some should not live.

And some foreigner now calling London his home,
From the great steppes of Russia to streets of old Rome,
Would come under suspicion as likely to be
Types who'd kill anybody they happened to see.

On and on went the talk as the liquor flowed hard.
There was great criticism toward Scotland Yard
As the London authorities struggled to cope
With the people of London's hard streets losing hope.

"Jack lives at the Palace." Holmes heard someone say,
*"And The Yard's been warned off, for it's always the way
Of those well-padded Royals to protect their own -
Their contempt for the poor of the city's well-known."*

Sherlock listened for hours but heard not a clue.
Any mob from the pubs would be hard to subdue.
He listened to all allegations that came
But was ever so grateful he'd not heard his name.

He heard nothing about anyone who'd been hurt;
Nobody, not one of the drinkers would blurt
Out the name of somebody they heard Jack had tried
To despatch with his knife but, with luck, hadn't died.

He must hope his friend Watson would have better luck.
But, for now, Sherlock Holmes, to escape, had to duck
All the jibes and the shoves of the drinkers aroused
By their liquor and talk as they wildly caroused.

He made no sudden moves but progressively shifted
His form to the doorway but found himself lifted
Aloft by a pair who went on the attack
Saying, *"This is none other than Whitechapel Jack."*

Sherlock kept his composure and acted the drunk
And was dropped by the pair. He recovered and slunk
His way out of the pub, the last one on his list,
And made way home to Baker Street through a thick mist.

There was danger for Holmes on each dark dingy street
For a man out alone had to hope he'd not meet
Vigilantes abroad looking out for Old Jack -
If some came upon him, they might well attack.

And Policemen, in force, would be out and about.
If one whistle was sounded, he'd hear the great shout
Of *"Stop right where you are. Don't you dare run away."*
But Holmes, in disguise and about, couldn't stay.

Sherlock had undertaken to not venture out
Onto Whitechapel streets – such an action would flout
The firm word that he'd given to colleague and friend
And he'd hate to be caught in a lie in the end.

Well aware, was the man, that some thought it may be
Jack the Ripper would turn out none other than he,
Sherlock Holmes, the grand master of plot and disguise -
To be caught on the streets would not be very wise.

But he knew that some risk by someone was required
And, though venturing out was an act undesired,
There was only one way that Old Jack would be caught
To be dragged where a lesson in hemp may be taught.

"Gather data," he'd say, *"if it's knowledge you seek.*
For the battle is lost if it's left to the meek
Who would stay behind doors, beneath bedcovers hide,
While great evil goes forth in the darkness outside."

Holmes had acted the drunk and had learned not a thing.
Not a hint had he heard of a clue he might bring
To his colleagues relying on his astute mind.
As a vicar, would he find a talkative kind?

That was something he'd try if John Watson had failed
To discover the name of that victim assailed
On that very first night of the dreadful attack
On the peace of the city by Whitechapel Jack.

It would take Holmes some time to return to the place
Where the friar was waiting and ready to face
What his friend had discovered – his mind was prepared
To receive any news – he was nervous, not scared.

Holmes walked briskly along every dark misty street
And few venturesome souls, on his way, would he meet
As the city closed doors on the danger which walked
In the person of Jack as, his victims, he stalked.

After hours, Holmes found himself turning the lock
Of his door as he heard, from the vestibule clock,
That the hour was Three and his knowledge had not
Been increased one iota – a damnable blot.

He ascended the stairs and he entered his rooms
To be greeted by snuffles and echoing booms
As his two friends slept, snoring, awaiting the man
Who had gone to Whitechapel despite Lestrade's ban.

Both awoke when he entered and asked if success
He had come to report or if he might confess
That no data was gathered – Holmes stated, "*I must
Admit that I have failed. My disguise, I'll adjust.*"

The Sleuth gave an account of his night's escapade
And how he had felt quite obliged to evade
The Police, Vigilantes and drink-driven Mobs
As he made his way home from his fact-finding jobs.

He would keep on explaining how he must be blamed
And how he, Sherlock Holmes, was completely ashamed
That he'd naught to report – both his friends interjected
Saying that the first victim may have been detected.

That same night, Watson visited colleagues and found
That, indeed, a poor woman had been brought around
With her hand slashed quite badly to Dr McBride
Who had treated her injury, he would confide.

McBride said that she'd cut herself badly on glass
From a smashed window pane upon trying to pass
Out a bottle of spirits to friends in the street -
She was shaken and bloodied and white as a sheet.

"Her name, she had given as Dot," McBride claimed,
*"And, though being badly cut, she at least wasn't maimed
For all tendons were missed. She examined his stitches
And laughed saying that they were sailors' half-hitches."*

"Well done," exclaimed Sherlock, *"this may be the clue
Which all London's been waiting for. We must pursue
This unfortunate woman and move her with speed
To a place where her safety can be guaranteed."*

"Well, we first have to find her." John Watson declared,
*"For, if she's been attacked and her life has been spared,
She is sure to be hiding and would be unwilling
To show herself until Old Jack stops his killing."*

*"It may be that Dot's not the woman's real name
For, if she is this victim, I'd offer no blame
For her keeping quite mute and away out of sight.
Were I her, I'd be hidden away every night."*

"*Sound thinking.*" said Sherlock, "*I don't disagree*
But we do need the woman who managed to flee
From the clutches of one who's determined to kill.
She has information so, find her, we will."

"*We must visit McBride for what more the man might*
Recall of this poor woman who put up a fight
When confronted by Jack and who laughed at the way
That her wound had been stitched in a nautical way."

"*She's a woman of spirit, but injured, no less,*
And she might be the type, with no overt duress,
To assist us in capturing Whitechapel Jack
Just as long as she's certain he will not come back."

"*But what of Lestrade? We must make a report.*"
Watson said with insistence, "*You know he's the sort*
Who'll insist that you honour the word that you gave.
It is he who lets you have that freedom you crave."

"*I concur with the Doctor.*" the friar asserted,
"*Inspector Lestrade should be duly alerted.*
There's no point in heroics, My Friend, for I know
That, your keenness to act, you are ready to show."

"*That is very commendable, but you've agreed*
That the way to catch Jack is by knowing what deed
He is apt to commit. The Police have the numbers
To cover the region the fellow encumbers."

THE RIDE

"Get some sleep." said the friar, *"Tomorrow we must*
See Lestrade and divulge what we know, though I trust
You will not let him know that this night you had slunk
To the pubs of Whitechapel dressed up as a drunk."

"That's today," added Watson, *"It soon will be dawn*
And, if you are like me, you'll be starting to yawn.
So we must get more kip for the dawning well may
Be the start of a trying and troublesome day."

Off to sleep went the trio, Sherlock stretching out
On the well-depressed sofa, still thinking about
What might lay before them when dawn finally broke.
For the first time in days Holmes had no need to smoke.

Having breakfasted early, the trio emerged
And, onto a four-wheeler, they quickly converged
And demanded the cabbie should find Scotland Yard
Without talk or delay – *"Get your team running hard."*

On the cold streets of London, the cab made its way
Through the mad crush of wagons determined to stay
On their well-travelled courses to market and dock -
Scotland Yard came in view as it struck eight o'clock.

"Well done, My Good Fellow. A guinea you'll earn
If you stand here and wait while we go in and learn
What we must be about. Very soon we'll have need,"
Sherlock said to the cabbie, *"of daring and speed."*

"I'll wait." said the cabbie, *"My team needs a rest*
After racing through London – they'll be at their best,
These two horses of mine – they'll be rested and fed
And be willing to run till their sides run with red."

"Good Man." shouted Holmes, *"Half a Crown on account*
And a good many more you'll be able to count
When your horses are stabled this day, after dark."
Sherlock threw him the coin without further remark.

The cabbie stepped down as the trio walked on
Through the Scotland Yard gate and inside, whereupon
They would seek out Lestrade and tell him of their news
And discuss what was learned and their relevant views.

Bert the Cabbie, meanwhile, thought it time to proceed
Fitting nosebags he always kept filled up with feed
Over each horse's nose – every horse has to eat,
And so Bert's well-fed horses were given a treat.

Bert would let them chew oats, a full portion for each,
Till the nosebags were empty and then he would reach
And remove them and place them away and then guide
Both to water the nearest horse-trough could provide.

As each horse drank its fill, Bert remarked to the pair
That, *"The fellow who paid us, the one with the flair,*
Was none other than he, Sherlock Holmes, on a case
So I think, My Two Friends, we are in for a chase."

Bert knew well such a client might want him to stand
Just ten minutes or so or, perhaps, might demand
A full hour or more – his reward would be such
That a cabbie like him would not care very much.

With his team of two horses all watered and fed,
Bert saw where in the street he could wait, so he led
Them to where they'd be seen, just not too far away,
For he knew that, such clients, he could not delay.

There was nothing to do for the cabbie but wait,
So he sang to his horses, not such a strange trait
For a man used to queuing for hours on end
Till the time when the clients, en-masse, would descend.

This was restful for him, and the horses, likewise.
He'd need all of his strength for the grand enterprise
He assumed was ahead – he left clients enraged
When he said, *"I can't take you. I'm fully engaged."*

In The Yard, quite excited, the trio sat down
Till Lestrade was available; then saw him frown
As he entered the room after being reproved
Once again for inaction – *"Get Jack or get moved."*.

*"This had better be good, for the end of my tether
It seems I have reached and I do not know whether
I'll be here tomorrow and filling this seat."*
Said Lestrade, *"Being fired might well be a treat."*

"We have news." stated Sherlock, *"That is, Watson may
Have detected the woman who'd gotten away
From the clutches of evil, that Whitechapel Jack.
We could use your assistance to get on her track."*

*"May have detected? Just what does that mean?
Do you know where she is? If you do, we must lean
On her gently or otherwise."* said the Inspector.
"If she helps us catch Jack, I will be her protector."

*"We have little to add at this time, but a friend
Of John Watson, a doctor, was called on to mend
A deep slash in the hand of a woman named Dot."*
Replied Holmes, *"That's all, at this time, we have got."*

"A small medical clinic in Middlesex Street
Is attended by Dr McBride for discreet
And affordable treatment for those who don't trust
London Hospital's doctors – his work is a must."

"We are now on our way to see Dr McBride
And, if you would be willing to come for a ride,
We've a cab outside waiting – the cabbie's been told
That the day may be one fit for only the bold."

"McBride's there till Eleven – we cannot waste time
For his treatment is free and his hours are prime.
He may well know this Dot and where she may be found
And she may help us run her attacker to ground."

"It's the hint of a clue, not a full clue as such,
But I'd like to come with you, Sherlock, very much.
I'll grab Gregson, he'll want to be in on this too."
Said Lestrade, *"And I need to get out of this zoo."*

Lestrade and the trio, with Gregson in tow,
Hurried out to the cabbie there waiting to know
Just what game was afoot and what quarry was sought -
He would help the Great Sleuth for a guinea or nought.

"Call me Bert, Mr Holmes. For one guinea, or none,
Tell me where we must go, tell me what you'd have done,
And we'll go there and do it, whatever it be.
My horses are ready – the same goes for me."

"Well said, Cabbie ..er.. Bert, we must be on our way
For there's much to accomplish on this very day."
Answered Sherlock, unsure what the cabbie might know,
"We are five who need speed so you should not go slow."

"Get you in, all you five, and just name any street
In the breadth of this city – I have yet to meet
Anyone who knows better this London of mine."
Said Bert, *"And we'll get there come rain or come shine."*

"You may take us to Middlesex Street, My Good Man."
Said Lestrade to the cabbie, *"As quick as you can*
For we've no time lose – it's official, you know,
And we're on Police business - no need to go slow."

Bert the cabbie watched all of his clients jump in
His four-wheeler and then, with a shout and a grin,
He announced to his horses that they could now start
A fast trot, then a gallop – he bid them, *"Depart."*

And, depart, they both did pulling hard on their load
At the word from their master – no need for the goad
For this team used to plodding the long London streets.
The five men inside went as white as new sheets.

Holmes recovered and said to the other four there,
"I did say that our cabbie would go anywhere
At a pace unrestrained by what might be called Law -
Once started, I fear it's too late to withdraw."

"Well, it's action, at least – I could do with the change."
Said Lestrade back to Sherlock, *"Do you think it strange*
That I need some excitement, and even some fear;
My pulses need racing, my head needs to clear."

"I've been sitting for weeks in that office of mine,
Checking rumours and letters from some asinine
And degenerate waster, or getting abused
By the Public, the Press, and my boss, unamused."

"Let the horse have its head, both the horses, that is.
Give the cabbie free-rein, for the horses are his
And he's off with us all – I'd not get in his way.
I've a feeling we may just get somewhere today."

But the galloping lasted a few minutes - just
Enough time to get everyone feeling they must
Be involved in a race – all their woes they forgot
Till the traffic in London demanded a trot.

"He is doing quite well, this fine cabbie you hired.
He has daring and nerve of a sort that's required
For the speed we must make." said Lestrade, *"And I'd say*
That the fellow is making amazing headway."

"All those on The Embankment are wondering why
Any cab such as ours would be needing to fly.
If they knew of our quest they'd be flying as well
But, of course, at this moment, we've little to tell."

"For the briefest of moments, I saw flashing past,
Our New Scotland Yard building, an edifice vast
And so very impressive – if I was a crook
I would get me arrested to have a good look."

"That's a bit optimistic," said Gregson, amused,
"But I'm sure that it will, in due time, be well used.
Did you hear, Mr Holmes, what the workers discovered?
A body chopped up – those men haven't recovered."

"A body? But, when?" Sherlock shouted, surprised
That he'd seen no report. *"Had nobody advised*
The newspapers that something like this had transpired?
They will say that, to hush it all up, you've conspired."

"*Well, there's some truth in that, I am forced to admit,*"
The policeman conceded, "*When it comes down to it,*
We did not want it linked with these Whitechapel crimes.
For us coppers, these are quite the queerest of times."

"*There were some similarities, that is quite true,*
But the body's location says we must pursue
Yet another disturbed and degenerate crook,
Though it might be for somebody sane we must look."

"*Someone sane? Is that so?*" broke in Watson, surprised,
"*I had thought all along that it had been surmised*
That a madman was loose with a motive arcane.
Sherlock said all along Old Jack isn't insane."

"*Well, maybe he is sane – if he is, he will hang*
When we catch him, and any he has in his gang
If he truly has help as those letters suggest."
Said Lestrade, "*But Jack's sanity's hard to digest.*"

"*I do think, with the timing and placement, we may*
Have a murder by someone who's hoping to sway
Our attention from him onto Whitechapel Jack.
This, I firmly believe, but it's clues that I lack."

"*Well, it's not a good omen for New Scotland Yard.*
A crime gone unsolved, you know, will be quite hard
For the Force to live down in those premises, new."
Sherlock commented wryly, "*Well, that is my view.*"

"*All these crimes, I admit, have us coppers on edge*
And we walk, every day, on a quite narrow ledge
With so many determined to watch if we slip
And a few who would purposely cause us to trip."

"We do question all villains in London we find
But, though some we suspect, most are not of a kind
Who would mutilate victims after an attack.
Most were bad, others mad, but not one was our Jack."

"Give me murder for profit or passion, I say."
Said Lestrade, *"I can understand murder for pay*
But I just cannot fathom this butcher called Jack.
Any sense of compassion, the fellow must lack."

"He kills for a reason," Friar Geoffrey declared,
"And a victim, once chosen will never be spared
For this man thinks he's righteous and quite justified
In the crimes he commits, though he's unsatisfied."

"Unsatisfied, Friar? Just what are you saying?
I mean no offence but I think all that praying
And banging of chests must be hard on the mind."
Quipped Lestrade trying hard not to be too unkind.

"I believe in great evil," the friar replied,
"And the fact that so many poor women have died
In the way that they did with their corpses defiled
Says that Jack is a man who, with death, is beguiled."

"He knows just what he's doing – he revels in it
And I fear that the man will be cast to The Pit
If God's judgement is thus – you seek him for The Rope
But, that he might surrender, is my forlorn hope."

"I do fear for the worst but must hope for the best.
I believe that our time on this Earth is a test
Of our fitness to enter that kingdom so grand
But, to do so, the Lord, a good life, will demand."

"Jack will find that those Pearly Gates slam in his face
For, to get a reward, he is out of the race."
Added Gregson, thinking about every attack,
"If there's truly a Devil, then send him Old Jack."

"That's enough!" yelled Lestrade, *"Whether insane or not,*
This man has to be stopped, for his acts are a blot
On this city of ours – we can't hold up our heads
Till we've captured this fellow that everyone dreads."

"We are nearing the entrance to Middlesex Street
And I fear it's a horde that the fellow will greet.
I would say we're too many to all go inside
And hear what may be said by this Dr McBride."

"Perhaps Friar Geoffrey and Gregson should stay
In the cab while we hear what the man has to say.
Dr Watson's his colleague, I'm Inspector in charge,
And Holmes might detect what we miss, by and large."

"The time will soon come when we'll hear victim one
Tell us what Jack was like and just what she had done
To fight off her attacker – we might be in luck
And learn much about Jack, all because of her pluck."

"Lestrade," spoke up Watson, *"I know you're in charge*
But it just will not do if the three of us barge
In like bulls through a gate. We must offer, I'd say,
Reassurance and, any suspicions, allay."

"McBride may be cagey and not wish to tell
What he knows of his patient – he'd know very well
That she could be the bait up to which Jack would rise.
To say that we'd use her that way won't be wise."

"You must give your assurance that she won't be named
For, to speak for myself, I would not have her blamed
If she shied from an offer to help in our quest.
She is frightened and hurt so, use tact, I suggest."

The cab came to a standstill; John Watson jumped out
While both Holmes and Lestrade saw the man look about
Then step off to the clinic of Dr McBride
Saying, *"Come on, you pair, we are needed inside."*

The detectives then followed while checking around
For types looking suspicious, types who may be found
To be watching the clinic in case Dot came back
And who might send a message to Whitechapel Jack.

None were seen, so they both followed Watson and went
Right on in where McBride would refuse or consent
To divulge what he knew of a patient called Dot.
They would be understanding but, fail, they would not.

McBride was quite wise in the ways of the street
And knew that, with his patients, he must be discreet
Lest they learn to distrust him – but this time he knew
That he must be forthcoming – his options were few.

The murders must stop – that, he knew very well
And the only way that would occur was to tell
What he knew of the victim – her name, her address.
But it did not sit well with the man, he'd confess.

THE DOCTOR

McBride greeted John Watson as colleague and friend
But, for Holmes and Lestrade, he just couldn't pretend
That he wanted their presence – his patients might wince
At the sight of detectives – his words he'd not mince.

"I do know why you're here and I know it to be
A necessity forced on you all, and on me,
But my patients are nervous and can be quite vague
And they all fear authority more than the plague."

"You stand in the abyss which is London's great shame
In which people are trapped, so afford them no blame
If they fear and distrust you, you should be advised;
And, if they don't cooperate, don't be surprised."

"I've known murderers, many, from all walks of life
Who would strike with the cudgel or slash with the knife
But I'm after a man who kills Whitechapel's own,"
Said Lestrade, *"and his motives, so far, are unknown."*

"Not just in Whitechapel," McBride then replied,
"Some women in Spitalfields also have died
At the hands of this Jack who, I'm told, has such hate
He takes bits of his victims to eat off a plate."

"We don't know that is so, but it could be the case
That the man does take trophies of sorts for some base
And degenerate reason I can't comprehend,"
Said Lestrade to McBride, *"nor could ever defend."*

"I admit that my job makes the world seem a place
Full of killers and liars and cheats and I face,
Every day, from the Public, derision and scorn,
But to defend that Public I've solemnly sworn."

"I too can feel fear – I have felt it today.
When I stepped to the roadway I heard myself say,
'Lestrade, look about you – your eyes should be cast
Toward dangers which could make this day be your last'."

"So, if some people fear me, then let it be so
For that makes my life safe for the moment, and 'No'
I do not hate them for it, and should they have need
I'll defend them from danger with force and at speed."

"I'm not here for the Government, nor for the Queen,
But for those humble folk who I see in between
Their predation by villains and death from disease
So don't lecture me on London's poor, if you please."

"Jack the Ripper's their enemy, not this old cop,
And I'll do what is needed to make the man stop
But I need information, not hearsay and lies -
Some cops might not care but this one does, and tries."

"The job you do here is a marvellous thing
But it's many a felon who's known where to bring
Anyone who's been wounded when breaking the Law
But we leave you alone – from your doors we withdraw."

"This man standing here, Sherlock Holmes, is a friend
But he often takes action that's hard to defend
For a man sworn to uphold the Law, but I know
That he fulfils a need so, some patience, I show."

"I have need of your help and it's that which I ask
For I'm stuck with a galling and perilous task.
I have need to know more of that patient who came
Seeking help on the night Old Jack started his game."

"She's in danger while ever The Ripper is free
Just because she's the one who was able to flee
From his clutches, and like us, he'll think she'll possess
Many details about him he'd like to supress."

"We have much information but very few leads
And we're flooded with rubbish when anyone reads
Of another who's succumbed to death from that knife
Wielded by Jack the Ripper, that taker of life."

"She will be well protected – we'll guard her by day
And by night if she wants it – or send her away
To a place where she'll never be threatened by Jack.
When the danger is over, we'll bring her straight back."

"We can offer assurances and a reward
If she helps points that finger of fate out toward
This insufferable menace of Whitechapel's streets
Who, it seems, kills for pleasure, the women he meets."

"To love me or loathe me is your given choice
But, to be rid of this Master of Hate, raise your voice
And tell me what you can or be cast as the one
Who could help but did nothing to bring Jack undone."

"At least protect your patient, please, Dr McBride.
Let us give the protection the Force can provide.
She's in danger right now – Death is there at her back
And a second chance she'll never get from Old Jack."

All the while Holmes said nothing but listened and saw
The response of McBride as Lestrade tried to draw
Out whatever was known of this woman called Dot.
Jack the Ripper had failed, but forgotten, had not.

"If I may, please, Lestrade, I will offer to ask
My good brother, Mycroft, for his help in this task.
He's a force at Whitehall and has agents at hand
And has many safe houses all over this land."

"Scotland Yard and Whitehall – it's an offer, supreme,"
Said Lestrade, *"and I'd say we may scupper the scheme*
Of that scourge of all London, our Whitechapel Jack.
We will only be safe when we hear his neck crack."

"I'm a healer, a fixer of bodies, you know."
Said McBride to Lestrade, *"So I hope you will show*
Some restraint to a madman, even to this Jack.
As for Dot, I must tell you great detail I lack."

"But I'm sure Dot's her name – I have seen her before.
She has brought sailors to me all covered in gore
After fights on the docks left their blood running free.
She's a woman of spirit, I'm sure you'd agree."

"But her surname? I only write down what they say,
All these patients who come, for I feel it's the way
To encourage them on to lead healthier lives;
One will only succeed if, for such things, one strives."

"I believe it is Sapper or Strapper, or such,
For she told me when bringing a man who made much
Of his pain, yelling out and in abject distress -
I do not keep good records, sometimes, I confess."

"I stop all the bleeding and, stitches, apply
To a neck or a belly and have to rely
On what patients might tell me – the truth it may be
But I know the majority tell lies to me."

"That is not my concern and, no questions, I ask.
To give medical help to the sick is my task
And I can't become known as a snitch for the Yard -
That would make my continued existence quite hard."

"Here's her card – not much on it, as is plain to see.
It records a Dot Sapper, which may or not be
Her real name, though I am fairly sure that it's Dot
But, to say where she lives, I'm afraid I cannot."

"Five stitches I had to insert in a gash
In the palm of her hand – it looked like a knife slash.
It will heal in time and, besides being scarred,
Her hand, upon healing, will not be left marred."

"She's supposed to come back – I believe that she might
For she wasn't the sort who would give in to fright
Or to panic and hide – if you find her she could
Say to leave her alone and, to do so, you should."

"But, conversely, she may go along, not to flee
Nor to hide, but you may find that she would agree,
With a little incentive, to join the attack
As the bait in a trap for this Whitechapel Jack."

"She lives down near the docks – she'd a reason to speak
While I gave that deep gash of hers a good tweak
While I cleaned it – it must have hurt like the blazes;
The fact that stood it just simply amazes."

"I'd forget the name Sapper – just ask all around
At the docks for a woman called Dot – she is bound
To be known by somebody along Cable Street -
Don't come on like Policemen or, Dot, you'll not meet."

Watson spoke for the group saying, *"Dr McBride,*
We appreciate what it took you to provide
Information on patients – in general, we'd not
Have expected that you'd give out any on Dot."

"It normally wouldn't be proper, you know,
And it's only to stop further harm that I'd show
You my notes," said McBride, *"but it just had to be.*
I don't wish Dot to learn you got her name from me."

"Now, folks come to this clinic for treatment, so one
Of you must make it look as though something was done
So I'll ask Mr Holmes that he hold out a hand
And I'll wrap the thing up with a dressing quite grand."

"It must be quite conspicuous, so he should keep
His hand raised up in front as if he'd been cut deep
And had come to be stitched, as so many have been -
It is well to look injured if, leaving, he's seen."

"That Lestrade brought you to me, somebody will know
And will also have seen you had Watson in tow;
You being seen to be injured provides an excuse -
The people 'round here, although poor, aren't obtuse."

"I will send you away looking like I've repaired
Some unfortunate injury which had impaired
An inquiry into some case, as a ruse -
Your friends brought you here and I couldn't refuse."

"Now, if Dot turns up here, I will tell her you asked
For a woman who had seen The Ripper unmasked
And was injured, perhaps, while escaping the fray -
I'll suggest that she seek Sherlock Holmes right away."

"Well, thank you, indeed." Sherlock said, *"Go ahead
And pretend that you've just taken needle and thread
And stitched up that deep wound I pretended to get -
You can tie a good bandage, McBride, I would bet."*

"It's a wager you'd win." said the Doctor as he
Began wrapping Holmes' hand so that Sherlock could be
Seen as patient attending, not sleuth on a case.
The three visitors left and went back to the chase.

Friar Geoffrey and Gregson had waited with Bert
Who had tended his horses while keeping alert
For the signs of the toughs who might rob a man blind -
Bert knew these streets well and knew they were unkind.

A sigh of relief he gave out upon seeing
His passengers hurrying, seemingly fleeing
Some trouble unseen, but then found he was rushed
To get going as, into the cab, they all crushed.

"Where to?" Bert demanded, and got the reply
That to Sullivan's Tavern they needed to fly
And discuss how they ought go about finding Dot -
Sherlock said that, to place her at risk, they could not.

Fifteen minutes would see them at table inside
And preparing to lunch with a drink and decide
The best way to proceed, to get her to respond
And agree to help out, not to make her abscond.

The discussions went on for an hour and more
As the five men went over at least a full score
Of the ways which might tempt Dot to join in the fight
And help bring her attacker out into the light.

They decided, at length, that the word should be spread
That somebody called Dot who someone wanted dead
Was being sought by a doctor called Watson who'd pay
For her story if she'd contact him right away.

She should send word that she might be willing to give
Her account of what happened, if she might relive
The events of that frightening night when she came
Face to face with a monster she wouldn't dare name.

She should send off a message to find Watson who
Would wait for her where ever she said he ought to.
He'd discuss, in the open, her options then say
She was really being sought for a plot now in play.

So the word was put 'round with the way to contact
Dr Watson – they hoped that this Dot would react
In the way that they wanted then not disappear
Upon hearing the plan – it was their greatest fear.

They knew this might alert Jack the Ripper, and he
Might keep watch upon Watson, arranging to be
Right behind him when he went to meet up with Dot
And so Watson must seek out a new secret spot.

Bert the Cabbie agreed to be in on the scheme
Which might be become dangerous in the extreme;
He would pick up John Watson where ever and when
Called upon and transport him – the man was a gem.

Sherlock had asked Mycroft if he might provide,
For a few days or weeks, somewhere Watson might hide
Till the time had arrived for his meeting with Dot -
To refuse to help Watson, Mycroft said he'd not.

With Watson ensconced and the word put around,
Watson waited impatiently, much like a hound
On a very short leash just awaiting the call
Out to action to start Jack the Ripper's big fall.

Two days went by slowly, that's what it would take
But John Watson could not go outside to partake
Of those streets he liked walking – he had to await
Any message from Dot. Would she rise to the bait?

That question was answered when Dot wrote to say
That she'd meet Dr Watson the very next day
At the middle of Waterloo Bridge right at Ten.
He must come in a cab; she'd bring someone called Ben.

On receiving the word, Watson shouted, *"At last!*
We'll have something to go on – the die may be cast
For this Whitechapel Jack." then made ready to act.
Dot must hear their offer – he had to use tact.

With Lestrade notified and Gregson on alert,
Sherlock sent out a message which told cabbie Bert
To pick up Dr Watson who'd then tell him where
He would want to be taken and transport him there.

At precisely nine-thirty, John Watson would stand
At the corner of Arundel Street and The Strand
Where a cab would arrive and he'd step on inside,
Settle down and relax for this critical ride.

At a distance discreet, Holmes would follow his friend
In a cab, with the friar, in case they must lend
Any needed assistance should things go awry -
Holmes could not get involved but at least he could spy.

His concern, most of all, was for this fellow Ben
Who was coming with Dot – was he one of the men
Who had helped Jack the Ripper and now threatens Dot?
Holmes thought on the matter but felt Ben did not.

More likely than not was that Ben was some friend
Or a husband or brother who'd come to defend
Dot against any danger which might come her way
For, her fears of attack, she would have to belay.

THE BAIT

In the morning, John Watson arose after Six
And considered the coming events with a mix
Of excitement and qualified anticipation
Although he'd admit to some slight trepidation.

He, too, had concerns of this Ben who'd escort
Dot to Waterloo Bridge – he'd received no report
From Lestrade or from Holmes on his identity
But dismissed any fears of Dot's duplicity.

Having broken his fast, Watson settled to read
All the papers he could – all the while he would plead
For the time to go faster – he'd hours before
He could get about doing his devious chore.

He did not like the fact that a lie had been told
On behalf of himself and that soon would unfold
The real reason Dot was being drawn out of hiding
From sanctuary, safe, where she had been residing.

But he steeled himself for the upcoming task,
Justifying the lie knowing it might unmask
Jack the Ripper and blunten that deadliest blade.
He'd hope Dot and Ben would forgive the charade.

The clock finally proclaimed that the hour of Nine
Had arrived and, by bracing his soldierly spine,
Dr Watson stood up, donned his coat and his hat,
Checked his pistol for bullets and, once again, sat.

Fifteen minutes would pass before he would proceed
To meet Bert and his cab, as it had been agreed,
On the corner of Arundel Street and the Strand -
It was always the waiting he found hard to stand.

He pondered on how he and Sherlock had pounced
After waiting for hours and how they had trounced
Many devious felons who hadn't prepared
For the crime they committed, and had them all snared.

But this time they were only collecting the bait
In a dangerous game in which one had to wait
For the quarry to blunder and not see the snare
And the bait to cooperate when made aware.

"She knows you as John Watson, a writer of tales,
And might think that her story might lead to more sales
And some cash back to her." Watson thought as he sat,
"But she must know of Sherlock – she may smell a rat."

"But, if that is the case, why would she risk a ride
In the centre of London which might well provide
A renewed opportunity for an attack,
If the word had leaked out, by this Whitechapel Jack?"

"Perhaps she is due far more credit than we
Have extended towards her – it's possible she
Has seen right through our ruse and is coming to get
Sherlock Holmes on the case – she may help us out yet."

Fifteen minutes passed by – Watson got to his feet
And proceeded to start for the place where he'd meet
Bert the Cabbie to go to meet Dot and this Ben -
Holmes would follow discreetly with several armed men.

Onto Waterloo Bridge, the cab, at a slow trot,
Proceeded with Bert looking out for this Dot
And her friend who'd be waiting – a couple they'd be.
Watson thought of success and of catastrophe.

A couple, Bert spied, and he tapped on the roof
Of his cab, all the while looking very aloof
But he pulled on his reins when the man at the spot
That the note specified yelled out, *"This cab for Dot?"*

"Yes, indeed." Bert replied, *"The good Doctor's inside*
And, if you'd get in with him, we'll have a good ride
Till I'm told where we're going, my cab and its fare.
That, you all must agree on, as I am aware."

Watson opened the door of the cab and then showed
Dot his face, so well known; and as Bert had now slowed
And had come to a stop Watson bid them *"Come in,*
We should get off this bridge before we would begin."

In both Dot and Ben hopped and the cab gave a jolt
As Bert signalled his team it was time they should bolt
From this place so conspicuous lest Dot be seen
In the open by Jack who, to find her, was keen.

Off at speed went the cab with its passengers, three,
Watson looking at Dot and at Ben hoping he
Could convince both of them to partake in a scheme
Which would end the short reign of a killer supreme.

He would say that he did have a story to tell
But the time wasn't right so, for now, he would quell
The temptation to offer the Public the story
Of murders so vile and so bloody and gory.

"Given all of the suffering and all the fear
Generated by Jack, my position is clear -
I must hold back my pen and ask help of you, Dot,
And of Ben, if he'll help in a devious plot."

The pair looked right at Watson in silence and then,
At each other, directed their gazes till Ben
Spoke up saying, *"We were not sure what to expect*
But we did, we admit, something deeper, suspect."

"Though it's not what the message had offered Dot, we,
That is, Dot has considered this meeting to be
By way of opportunity placed in her way
To remove Jack the Ripper and make the man pay."

"So, if there is some plan to snare Whitechapel Jack,
We would like to hear more – I hear his last attack
Was so brutal that many could not bear to look
On the form of the victim while hardy men shook."

Watson looked at the pair and then gave each a smile,
Gratified that he hadn't resorted to guile
More than putting his name to a message to draw
Dot from hiding – such deception would stick in his craw.

"What you say is quite true, I am forced to admit,
But before saying more, and if you would permit,
I must offer you transport, privacy to restore,
Or proceed to a place where it's safe to talk more."

"Well, proceed as you will, Dr Watson, for we
Haven't come all this way for a ride just to be
Taken back where we started." said Ben, in a tone
Of determined resolve, *"Let me get Jack alone."*

"By the way," broke in Watson, *"The lady .. well, Dot,*
And yourself, that is, Ben, you're a pair, are you not?"
"Yes we are," replied Ben, *"and we're seven years wed*
And from trial and trouble we never have fled."

"Dot and Ben, that we are, and Sapper is our name.
I had worked on the ships till my Dot here became
My good wife, and a true one with her golden locks.
Now I work as a trader right down on the docks."

"We can make a good living – our time is our own
And our name, in some quarters, is one which is known
For straight dealing and fairness - our measures are just
And our business is run via handshakes and trust."

"But this creature, so vile, who the people call Jack
One night took it upon him to up and attack
My good Dot as she turned down our very own street -
He did not expect, such a fighter, to meet."

"He went off at a run but Dot's hand had been cut
Rather badly and she hurried home safely, but
I was off doing business that very same night
Otherwise I'd have been there and she'd be alright."

"I returned the next day – we saw Dr McBride
And we thought to report the attack and provide
What we could, when we heard of the savage attack
In Whitechapel and thought that we ought to hold back."

"With that man on the loose, we decided to stay
In our home and in safety till he went away.
In hindsight that was foolish but fear for dear life
Made me overprotective of Dot, my dear wife."

"This Jack might live near us, that was out main thought,
And if he knew that Dot was the victim he sought
He might well seek her out and, well, finish what he
Had begun, and I could not let that come to be."

"As the murders continued, we knew we should speak
But the thought of this man killing Dot made me weak
And I say, to my shame, I did not say a thing
But just locked all my doors and, to safety, I'd cling."

"But this last grisly murder had left us unnerved
And we wondered if us staying mute even served
The designs of The Ripper, but then we were told
Of the search for some Dot and of tales to be sold."

"We decided right then that we had to come out
From behind our locked doors and tell you about
What had happened. But how did you know about Dot?
We told no one about it – to risk that, we'd not."

"We shall talk about that in good time when we meet
With some people who will be extremely discreet
About who they have spoken to and what's agreed."
Stated Watson, insistent, *"And what you might need."*

"Can your business stand being left idle for now
Or must you be about it? We'd like to know how
You might feel about leaving your post at this time.
Your business is merchandise, we battle crime."

Ben thought hard about this and he said, *"Well, I'd say,*
As the docks are now quiet, I could be away
For a fortnight or more, then I ought to get back -
Ships must get on unloading in spite of this Jack."

"That could work in our favour, it could work in well
If the word got about that you'd gone for a spell
To the country or off for a visit to see
Your old mother, or someone." Watson said with glee.

"Well, I do have a brother in Henley who I've
Not been able to see in an age, though we strive
To communicate often by mail. I could send
Him a telegram, if that's what you'd recommend."

"That is an idea, although things might unravel
Unless we act swiftly – perhaps you might travel
To Henley, forthwith." Watson said to his charge,
"You'll be out of harm's way while Old Jack is at large."

With a nod of agreement, Ben looked right at Dot
Saying, *"It's a predicament, like it or not,*
But a break from this city is long overdue -
Dr Watson's advice may provide us our cue."

Watson said to them both, *"We shall drive to a place*
Where some people are waiting – the cabbie will trace
His way there, by and by – we are followed, you know,
By that man, Sherlock Holmes, with a few men in tow."

"The Police haven't asked for his help in a way
That's official, of course, but a plan's underway
For his talents, covertly, to be utilised
While the powers that be all remain unadvised."

"There is jealousy, rampant, abroad at The Yard
And those in high command have all made it quite hard
To have matters looked into by Holmes from the start."
Watson said, overlooking his causative part.

"We'll soon meet two Policemen, detectives they'll be,
Both official Inspectors who, with Holmes and me,
Will put forward a plan which may see Old Jack snared,
A plan which, in fact, has been partly prepared."

Watson opened the door of the cab and leaned out
And, as Bert leaned toward him, directions he'd shout
To the place where they'd meet to develop the plan
Of attack which would see Scotland Yard get its man.

As the cab turned a corner, the couple within
Saw upon Watson's face a broad unrestrained grin
As if telling them both that, with danger about,
They had chosen to face it, not seek a way out.

"I admire your spirit," the Doctor declared,
"It has made this land great; it is why we have fared
So remarkably well in a world filled with strife.
I admire you, Sapper – yourself and your wife."

"But enough of my prattle - it seems we've arrived
At our place of decision where planning, contrived
To bring Whitechapel Jack to the gallows, we'll make.
We must talk of the danger, of risks we must take."

At a secret location, the cab had arrived;
The Doctor, the husband, the wife who survived
A most deadly attack by man quite depraved
Who could only be beaten by danger being braved.

Without fanfare of fuss, from the cab they emerged
With their senses afire and a keenness which verged
On the point of excitement – they entered a door
To see two grim Inspectors both pacing the floor.

"Watson," one shouted, *"You've managed to bring
The first victim of Whitechapel Jack - everything
Which now happens will be on our own terms, not his.
We'll soon show him a gallows, the tallest there is."*

"First things first, I'll insist." Watson said just as Dot
Got her bearings within a dim room which had not
Seen a glimmer of sunlight in one hundred years,
"Light a lamp, will you Gregson, deliverance nears."

*"We've been waiting in darkness, just cooling our heels
While awaiting events – coppers know how that feels."*
Replied Gregson while striking a match on his boot,
"I've been pacing this floor like some silly galoot."

After Gregson had lit up the lamp, Watson told
His two charges they had come inside to behold
The Inspectors Gregson and Lestrade working hard
Bringing light to the darkness in spite of The Yard.

*"No more jokes, Dr Watson, The Yard has its ways
Which are proper and lawful, an operative strays
From the rulebook too far at great risk to his health,"*
Said Lestrade, *"not to mention wellbeing and wealth."*

"Introduce your new friends, Dr Watson, for we
Are quite anxious to learn how someone came to be
Left alive by The Ripper – she must have some pluck
Or be blessed by the angels or laden with luck."

"Or quite possibly all of the three attributes
You'd suggest describe Dot when she's having disputes
With a fiend who, upon spilling her blood, is intent."
Dr Watson broke in, *"She is magnificent."*

"But here, if I'm right, is Sherlock and a few
Men at arms, so to speak, who'd have left Jack askew
And disjointed somewhat should the man have attacked.
He'd have learned what it was to be beaten and hacked."

In came Homes and the friar, the extras outside
In case Whitechapel Jack had found somewhere to hide
And had followed along to discover the plot
Which might end with his neck in a tight hempen knot.

Then, as no one had followed, no one had been seen,
The gathered detectives said that they were keen
To find out what Dot knew of the man she had fought
And, though hurt, had beat off – her help they all sought.

Watson introduced Gregson, Lestrade and Sherlock
To both Dot and Ben Sapper who said, *"It's a shock*
To meet you, Mr Holmes – of your exploits, we've read -
How you've shown the Police the correct way ahead."

"Yes, he's a marvel." said Lestrade with a scowl,
Overcoming the urge to deliver a growl,
"Dr Watson would tell you that we, at The Yard,
Are just bumbling fools who it ought to discard."

"But this isn't the time such discussions should be
Brought to bear on the subject of just how should we
Go about catching Jack and preventing more death.
To do so at this point is waste of good breath."

"So, before we get into the details, I'd ask
If you're up for a possibly perilous task
Which calls on Mrs Sapper to sit and await
Jack the Ripper's advances by being live bait."

THE TRAP

All eyes fell upon Dot, ten for those who would know
If this injured survivor would possibly show
Inclination or not to draw Whitechapel Jack
To a trap from which he'd never find his way back.

Dot looked right at Ben and she nodded assent
And then Ben nodded back knowing that, to prevent
Further murders, ongoing, someone had to act
And do more than just hide - to take chances, in fact.

"I have told Dr Watson I'm up for a dare
And am fully prepared to give Jack a good scare,"
Declared Dot quite determined to have the man caught
Even though such a plan, with some danger, was fraught.

"Excellent!" said Lestrade, *"There are things I must ask*
Before things can be planned for this perilous task.
Tell us all that you can. Was the man short or tall?
Was he fat? Was he slim? If you know, tell us all."

"How was the man dressed? Could you say his accent
Sounded local or foreign, from Yorkshire, from Kent?
Did it sound educated - the gentry, perhaps?
Did it carry the ring of those Cockney-bred chaps?"

Dot considered the questions and said, *"Well, I'd say*
That he wasn't from London but somewhere away
To the north, by his accent, though his words were few
And I heard little after, that long knife, he drew."

"But he did yell, 'You harlot! To Hell I will send
You and many more like you till this land can mend
Its abominable ways.' and then I saw the knife
And I knew I was in for a fight for my life."

"I held up my hand as the man gave a slash
With that terrible knife – it came down in a flash
And I felt it cut right through the flesh of my palm.
It hurt quite a lot but somehow I stayed calm."

"He raised up his hand once again but I poked
My umbrella tip into his throat and he choked
Just enough to let me kick him where it would hurt.
Well, I cannot repeat what that caused him to blurt."

Lestrade gave out a laugh and said, *"Well done, My Dear.*
You did not go down passively, that much is clear."
"Inspector," she said, *"in his eyes, I saw hate -*
If I hadn't struck back he'll have sealed my fate."

"Six men, are we here, in this room and I'd say
That we all stand in awe of the spirited way
You struck back at this fiend," said Lestrade back to Dot.
"Your courage, few men could admit they have got."

"That's my Dot," added Ben, *"she has beauty and brains*
And the nerve of an Amazon, though she refrains
From displaying the latter unless she is riled.
She fought off this madman, this Jack we've reviled."

"Her hand's not fully healed and it will be a while
Before it should be used but, alas, it's futile
To tell her she must rest it and let the wound mend.
Dr Watson, can you say what you'd recommend."

Dr Watson grinned broadly and said, *"My Dear Chap,*
Mrs Sapper is like Sherlock Holmes in a scrap.
He will never be told, he'll not listen to me,
He's a law to himself and I must let him be."

"Jack the Ripper tried hard, you will have to admit,
To make your Mrs Sapper afraid and submit
To the point of his knife and she came out on top -
If I thought to instruct her, I'm sure she say 'Stop!'."

"Right you are, Dr Watson," Dot said in reply,
"Whether healed or not, I will certainly try
Anything to get back at this Whitechapel Jack -
Get me close to the man - I'll go on the attack."

"Well said." stated Watson and all there agreed
That the woman among them had courage, indeed,
But Lestrade broke in, saying, *"But, please, can you tell*
Anymore of this Whitechapel Jack sent from Hell?"

Dot replied with, *"Inspector, it was rather dark*
But there was a light glowing and making its mark
Just enough so that I could see where I was at.
Any less, I'd have needed the sense of a bat."

"My assailant was not all that tall, though not short,
And at first I had thought him a drunk after sport
Of scandalous nature – that type one can see
Every night of the week, full of drink, roaming free."

"The fog had begun to descend but was not
Very thick on that night, but the man was a blot
Till he got so much closer than what I would like -
Armed with my umbrella, his head I would strike."

"He wore some sort of cape, black or brown I would say;
It had some sort of hood, not a hat, in the way
That the nuns often wear at their prayers in the morn -
It's the sort which an olden-day monk might have worn."

"A monk much like me?" Friar Geoffrey then asked
As he walked into view like some phantom unmasked.
Dot gave out a loud *"You! I will cut you this time*
And you'll pay with your soul for each dastardly crime."

Dot then pulled out a knife with her uninjured hand
But Lestrade told her curtly, *"You must understand*
That this man's here to help us – he thinks he knows Jack."
Just as Friar Geoffrey took several steps back.

"He came down from the North just as soon as he saw
What the papers had written – it stuck in his craw
That he had not heard tell of the murders down South -
They recalled evil words from a former monk's mouth."

"Well, we feel very strongly Jack's known to this man,
Friar Geoffrey, who's travelled to do what he can
To prevent Jack's outrages on Whitechapel's streets.
Old Jack may well butcher each woman he meets."

"Or he might choose his victims to make them atone
For what he thinks they're up to by walking alone
In the dark of the night – he gets some sort of thrill
By pretending he's God and it's his right to kill."

"So please, Mrs Sapper, please tell us some more
Of the man who attacked you - you've told us he wore
What looked like a monk's habit and spoke in a way
Of a man of religion who'd gone far astray."

"Too far, I would say, also not far enough,"
Dot replied to Lestrade, *"for his justice is rough.*
And if God is on-high, let Him strike the man down -
There are innocent women all over this town."

"None deserve what he does, when alive or when dead."
Sherlock Holmes said to Dot and to all, *"In his head*
Is a game of some sort which he plays in a way
That makes him feel superior – that's what I say."

"He's pathetic, resorting to killing those who,
By their deaths and their suffering, turn him into
Some ridiculous knight on an errand to purge
Those who cannot fight back – it's a base coward's urge."

"Dr Watson can tell you, from women I draw
Well away from but not for some devious flaw -
I admire them greatly but, my mind, I've trained
And rejected romance and, from passion, refrained."

"I'm a thinking machine and emotions do not
Help the least when I'm solving some intricate plot
Which involves someone of that peculiar sex
Which I hold in esteem and consider complex."

"Detection's my calling, I must steer my mind
From the complications of the romantic kind.
It's a type of religion, this crime-fighting lark,
And it doesn't have room for a romantic spark."

"Dr Watson is quite the romantic, I'm told.
His desire for a lady's regard leaves me cold
But his heart is a true one, that is a plain fact
So, from being respectful, he cannot detract."

"But this man we are seeking is not of that kind;
He does have, I suspect, a superior mind
In a few of its aspects but, of women, he's scared
As seen how, when against Mrs Sapper, he fared."

"Well, scared, he may be, but there's hatred as well,
For the way that he butchered his victims should tell
Of his evil obsession." said Watson annoyed
By the way Holmes had, with his romantic side, toyed.

"This is prattle enough," said Lestrade with a growl,
"But we can't have this bird out at night like some owl
Seeking out a fresh morsel to jump on and kill,
Though owls hunt when they hunger and not for a thrill."

"We have little to go on although we can say
That Jack's dressed like a monk and has come from away
To the north, and he fancies himself quite proficient
At chess, though his logic is somewhat deficient."

"We don't know where he lives, how he dresses by day.
We don't know what he eats or if he's in the pay
Of someone very evil, far more than Old Jack.
We don't know if he's gone and will never come back."

"If the latter's the case, which I hope would be true,
We cannot just give up – all his victims are due
A full measure of effort; we're committed, in fact,
To have Old Jack atone for each barbarous act."

"Perhaps," said the friar, *"he's found his two friends*
And they're hiding somewhere in this city which lends
Itself to little scrutiny into these crimes
And they only go forth at their opportune times."

"Remember he spoke of his knights – this suggests
That man has his helpers or that the man jests
In a maddening way." Friar Geoffrey surmised,
"If those two monks were with him, I'd not be surprised."

"He may well be ensconced in a sect of some sort
Where he'd not be suspected but get the support
He would need to survive – one would never expect
That a monk was a menace, a Ripper suspect."

"There are so many places to hide, in that case,
But I do agree with you, such could be a base
For a monster well used to the cloistered domain."
Sherlock said to the friar, *"Much, this could explain."*

"But with railways abounding all over this land
There are places aplenty this hooded brigand
Might hold up in until he decides that it's time
To go forth and commit a contemptible crime."

"He might hide out in Oxford or Cambridge by day
And come down in the evening, perhaps, just to stay
Long enough to commit one more dreadful attack
And then, on the night train, go quietly back."

"But, of course, there are places apart from these towns
Full of priests and professors all dressed in their gowns
Where a man in a habit and hood might well hide -
Winchester and Canterbury, such could provide."

"And a good hundred more, I would say; but the blood
From the victims he's killed, on his habit, would flood.
He would never be able to step on a train
And, even if washed, some would surely remain."

"No, I think we must look for locations nearby
For a hiding place, holy, which would satisfy
All his bodily needs and a base for attack
In which none would suspect him of being Old Jack."

"That does make some sense, I'm inclined to agree,"
Said Inspector Lestrade, *"That would leave the man free*
To go forth any night and not have to depend
On the trains where, with lighting, he'd have to contend."

"So, Holmes, it would seem that a monk is our man
And is hiding nearby. Well, I'm sure that we can
Make inquiries, subtle, to find someone who
Might have recently joined them – it's what we must do."

"Well, of course, we must do that," said Holmes in reply,
"But I really do think we should not let on why
We are asking such questions – suspicion's not proof
And our man, if alerted, might prove quite aloof."

"If we do find a suspect, we must sit and wait
While we ready our hook with the right sort of bait.
Mrs Sapper has tensed up her every sinew -
Jack the Ripper may bite off more than he can chew."

"We must leak to the Press that a witness has told
Scotland Yard that a fellow, so callous and cold,
Had attacked and had cut her but she had survived
And her memory of him had now been revived."

"Lestrade will refuse to make comment upon
Any questions put to him – The Yard's lexicon
Full of jargon, official, will serve the man well -
But he will, to one journalist, have much to tell."

"Is there one you can trust to control his desire
To be first with a headline which might fan the fire
Away out of control when we just need a spark
To get Whitechapel Jack to come out of the dark?"

"Yes, there's one, but I daren't let the word get away
For my guts would be turned into garters that day
If the powers-that-be ever knew I had done
Such a dangerous thing – and, prospects, I'd have none."

"But that's what I hear daily from those up on high
At The Yard, and I must say I learned just to sigh
And insist that I'm doing as much as I can
To detect and to capture our Whitechapel man."

"You must use the term 'checkmate' in any report;
Not a thing, though, of bishops and knights - just resort
To that babble that only Policemen can do -
The Press will make ten out of just two and two."

"I assume, Friar Geoffrey, this will not offend
Any notions of honesty – I'd recommend,
If it does, that you leave us to fight as we may -
No hold will be barred when we get Jack at bay."

"A lie, an untruth, call the ruse what you will,
But the man will be thinking of blood he can spill."
The good friar replied with a mischievous grin,
"And deceiving the Devil cannot be a sin."

"Good Man!" said Lestrade, *"We could use your insight*
To locate Jack the Ripper and bring him to light.
Would you speak to the clergy of cloistered domain?
You will know what to say and from what to refrain."

"My time and my talents, and even my life,
Are all at your disposal – we must stop that knife
Cutting into more flesh." said the friar, prepared
To do what was required to have Old Jack snared.

"It do feel that I'm guilty, in some little way,
For not stopping this friar before he could stray
From our ancient enclosure where we he was contained
To a world unprepared for his acts unrestrained."

"I don't feel I'm to blame, but perhaps it is true
That I failed to act on an obvious clue,
Even though I knew nothing of any intent
To descend upon London and, great anger, vent."

Lestrade countered by saying, *"We Police feel that way*
After seeing events in the cold light of day
After things that might happen have turned into fact -
It is then that the critics get into the act."

"You ought have seen this and you ought have done that,
They will yell from the rooftops, like some cheeky brat
Who does nothing to help but insists that we take
Every risk that we can for his own safety's sake."

"It's the way of the world and it never will change;
When the people are safe, it's like we have the mange.
But, if ever some danger or trouble appears,
They're off under their blankets till everything clears."

"They expect we'll appear for the pittance they pay
And make all of their troubles go swiftly away.
But should this take some time, if a witness won't speak,
Then our efforts are labelled as useless and weak."

"There is nothing for which you should ever reproach
Yourself in such a way – you made every approach
When you learned of the facts – far more than most would,
And you've given us more than 'most anyone could."

"We'll do what Holmes suggested, we'll set up a snare
And we'll bait it, if she is still up for the dare,
With Dot, Mrs Sapper, who's given her all,
And this Menacing Monk will be set for a fall."

THE HOOK

Lestrade said to the group, *"It is time to depart*
For, if Whitechapel Jack is the merest bit smart,
He might know somethings on if, together, we're spotted.
We will meet up again when a time is allotted."

"We'll have Mr and Mrs Sapper taken to
A hotel for their safety – it's one which will do
For the moment until we can get them transferred
Out to Henley – I believe that is what they preferred."

"Tomorrow they'll go down to Paddington where
They will take the train right out to Twyford, and there
They will change for the branch line to Henley to meet
With Ben Sapper's good brother up on Friday Street."

"This is close to the station and, this time of year,
Any stranger approaching will stand out quite clear
As someone to be watched – we'll have people on guard
In the town, in the street and in Ben's brother's yard."

"The Sappers should go now in Bert's handy cab
While Gregson and myself will both, very soon, grab
Down the road a quick Hansom to take us to meet,
At their hotel, the Sappers – Gregson, move your feet."

"Perhaps Watson and Holmes and the good friar might
Wait a good half an hour before going right
Back to Baker Street where we shall all talk at length
Of the trap we would set, every weakness, each strength."

"I will be there tonight, though I could be quite late
For I know I am in for an extended spate
Of recriminant questions and threats of the sack
For not coming home with our Whitechapel Jack."

"I will have a man with me, a journalist who
Will, of course, understand what we're trying to do.
He's not in it for headlines – he's one man I trust
But, to let him print something, I definitely must."

"He will write how Police have been outfoxed by Jack
And The Yard should do more and get on the attack.
He will write how Inspector Lestrade has a plan
To checkmate Jack the Ripper and bring home his man."

"But we'll talk of this further tonight, after nine,
So get what rest you can and perhaps we can dine
On what Mrs Hudson would call one of her treats
After I've been reminded of all my defeats."

Off the group went in stages, the Sappers ahead
Of the tired Inspectors who wished they, instead
Of providing their charges with rest overnight,
Could go home to their beds to arise sharp and bright.

The Sleuth and the Doctor and Friar would stay,
As the trio was asked, till the rest got away.
Thirty minutes they waited, then Watson emerged
To engage a four-wheeler on which they converged.

"To Regent's Park, Cabbie, the Baker Street end,
You may take us and drop us just where the street bends.
You may hurry along or you may take your time,"
Uttered Watson, relaxed, *"for this night is sublime."*

Not a word about what was afoot would be spoken;
To do so would leave any secrecy broken.
Just the mention of Whitechapel Jack could result
In a shout of *"The Ripper!"* and massive tumult.

So they spoke very little and nothing of Jack
Till they, somewhat expectant, found that they were back
Near Two-twenty-one-B Baker Street where they might
Talk about Jack the Ripper all through a long night.

But Sherlock sat in silence and pondered upon
Lestrade who had behaved like a grand paragon
Taking charge in a manner he rarely had seen -
Though restricted by Law, Lestrade's manner was keen.

Mrs Hudson was called – they requested she serve
Up a marvellous supper for those who'd deserve
Special treats for their efforts, unseen and unknown -
Gregson and Lestrade such regard would be shown.

After nine, they would come; there were hours to fill
In what manner they could but they could not sit still.
They were hoping the Sappers were safely inside
Their hotel room with all the Police could provide.

The three men tried to sleep but could not settle down;
Sherlock filled up his pipe and ignited its crown;
Watson read his newspaper but drifted away;
Friar Geoffrey tried hard then decided to pray.

The time drifted along at a leisurely pace
Till at last Mrs Hudson's footsteps they could trace
On the steps coming up with hot tea in a pot
And a few meaty nibbles, not cold and not hot.

"This will keep you all going until they arrive,
Our Inspectors Lestrade and Gregson who'll revive
Both their bodies and spirit when eating my fare -
They'll not say they're not hungry, they better not dare."

"This is welcome, indeed, a repast fit for kings."
Declared Sherlock observing the delicate things
Of delectable nature his landlady brought,
"Mrs Hudson prepared them so, eat them, we ought."

And, eat them, they did with the greatest delight
And, within a few minutes, there wasn't the sight
Of a morsel remaining, no fragment or crumb;
Mrs Hudson looked on and was struck slightly dumb.

"Well, I must say you men like your food; it's a treat
To observe hungry people determined to eat
What I put on a plate," Mrs Hudson declared,
"I assume you enjoyed all those treats I prepared."

"Well, 'enjoy' is a word far too subtle to use
When your cooking's discussed, Mrs Hudson. A Muse
Must have taught you the way," Sherlock said with a grin,
"To make food for the gods of the heavens therein."

"I am spoiled." Friar Geoffrey declared just as he
Took another great bite, then he said, *"It could be*
That I'll have to account for indulgences keen
And admit to my brothers the glutton I've been."

"But a penance of prayer and a fortnight of gruel
Will get me in condition to keep up the duel
Against evil which I'll never cease to combat.
Mrs Hudson, I fear you are making me fat."

"You're as thin as a rake and you eat like a mouse."
Mrs Hudson then countered, *"When you're in my house*
You'll not go without food and you'll eat what you're fed.
Mr Holmes sometimes looks like the fellow's been bled."

"This tenant of mine often goes without food
And eats only, it seems, when he gets in the mood.
But I have to insist, as I do with that man,
That the guests of my tenants eat all that they can."

Watson gave out a laugh and he said, *"I would say,*
Sherlock Holmes eats so little a fellow could play
A fine tune on his ribs which must surely protrude."
Mrs Hudson broke in with, *"Now, that's a bit rude."*

The Sleuth grinned and replied *"A fine tune, I will play,*
On a trim violin which is fed, I would say,
On the food of Apollo, the musical god."
Watson and the friar both gave him a nod.

"I will listen downstairs, so a lyrical note
Is what I'll be expecting and on which I'll dote."
Mrs Hudson said softly while pouring more tea,
"But no discordant airs, that is my earnest plea."

"I'll be back about nine when more guests will arrive
And you'll have a fine supper for which I'll contrive
Something special – I do know Lestrade likes a treat
And I know what the fellow likes, mostly, to eat."

"He works very long hours, you should be aware
And, for regular meals, does not seem to care
Or does not get the chance when he's out fighting crime;
So, tonight, I do hope that he does take his time."

Mrs Hudson slipped out through the door and descended
The stairs after feeling that she had defended
Someone she had come to regard as a part
Of the Baker Street team, both hardworking and smart.

She thought Sherlock dismissed him too often as slow.
A consulting detective, she thought, ought to know
That his life was the Force and his time must belong
To the ones giving orders – to judge him was wrong.

Holmes took out his old violin and its bow
And took time to prepare it and also to show
Friar Geoffrey its features, explaining how he
And the music it made, in his youth, came to be.

"It relaxes my mind more than nicotine can
And it isn't as smoky – Watson has to fan
In fresh air from the window whenever I smoke.
Well played, violins will, the heavens, invoke."

Sherlock's playing, as well as the food they had eaten,
Had inner demons of the trio all beaten,
Defeated and shackled and chained up once more;
Too often they'd break free and come to the fore.

The clock chimed out Seven then Eight and then Nine.
Sherlock Holmes had stopped playing his music divine
When a cab had pulled up right outside in the street.
"I believe," Sherlock said, *"this is they we must meet."*

Holmes peered through his window, observing three men
Getting out of the cab and he saw Lestrade then,
As so often he'd done, walk on over and ring
On the doorbell announcing he'd news he must bring.

"It's Lestrade and it's Gregson and someone in tow,
Someone from the Press, I believe, are below
In the street seeking entry. Ah, there goes the door
And I hear a policeman's great boots on the floor."

Then a scuffle of boots made its way up the stairs
And, while Watson got busy distributing chairs,
Sherlock opened the door before Gregson could knock
Saying curtly, *"You're late, it is past nine o'clock."*

Gregson said, *"It's Lestrade, he always likes to be*
Just a little bit late – I have noticed that he
Likes to send us ahead, he makes it a demand,
And he then makes an entrance excessive though grand."

"Cut it out," said Lestrade, *"you're the bane of my life*
And you both contribute to a large share of strife
That I get in this job – I am not in the mood.
By the way, didn't somebody here mention food?"

"I've been at Scotland Yard eating crow off a plate
So forgive if I am a tiny bit late.
I have with me somebody to bring Jack undone -
He writes for a newspaper - well, you know the one."

"William Hooper, I don't know if you've ever met
Sherlock Holmes; this is he, and it is a good bet
That you'll know Dr Watson, he scribbles as well,
And meet Friar Geoffrey on whom misfortune fell."

"Yes, I've met Sherlock Holmes in the course of events
And also Dr Watson who often presents,
In his own unique style, their adventuresome tales."
Said Hooper, *"I often begrudge him his sales."*

"Yes, he takes good examples of logical thought
And he stretches the truth more than anyone ought
For an audience fickle." Holmes said with a sigh,
"I do not understand why his sales are so high."

"Well, the Public," said Hooper, *"I'll tell you, does not*
Care a fig for the truth but wants all that you've got
Of suggestions of scandal and stories with gore,
And that Public so fickle will clamour for more."

"There's a lifespan for stories, they're born and they die;
They grow up and mature and then fade, and we vie,
In the Press, to report what we can in a way
That will keep us in business at least one more day."

"Numbers, Mr Holmes, they allows us to live
And to sell advertising space so lucrative
But also quite competitive that we must move
Our newspapers in ways of which some disapprove."

"I could write up a story to say how you saw
Through a quite clever ruse by detecting a flaw.
But if I told the Public a minister's wife
Had run off with her lover, the sales would be rife."

"But we're not here to banter, we're here to incite
A despicable fellow whose mad appetite
Both for murder and mayhem has driven up sales.
Perhaps we can bait him with one of our tales."

"We're a massive machine, Mr Holmes, that exists
And it talks to the Public which rarely resists
What gets printed on pages it's fed every day.
It's a word-hungry world and we won't go away."

"Inspector Lestrade's filled me in on events
Which your friar reported amid great laments
For the clues that he missed even though it's been shown
That the crimes, when committed, to him were unknown."

"He has spoken of chess and the taunts from Old Jack
And it has been suggested we send him one back
In a 'roundabout way hoping that he will bite -
It's hoped this would whet the man's mad appetite."

"Well, while appetite's on the agenda, I'd say
That I hear Mrs Hudson – she's headed our way
With a supper like none, all your life, you have had."
Watson said, breaking in, saying, *"Time to eat, lad."*

Six men salivated on what they next saw
Although, drooling the most, were the men of the Law.
The aroma hit Hooper as upward it rose -
He stopped talking as soon as it entered his nose.

"Mrs Hudson, I love you. You're just the best cook
And this meal you've prepared, I must say, has the look
And aroma which chefs would be hard pressed to match."
Said Lestrade thinking hard onto which he'd first latch.

There was coffee aplenty to go with the food
For, although they'd gone into a most festive mood,
They would soon settle down to discuss just how they
Could convert Jack the Ripper into easy prey.

And, discuss things, they did till the clock sounded Twelve;
They'd drunk pots full of coffee contriving to delve
Into just what might trigger The Ripper to rise
To a bait on a hook and to cause his demise.

Hooper wrote many versions till all had agreed
That the hook was quite sharp and would likely succeed
When the quarry bit hard as they all hoped he would -
On this night the six men had done all that they could.

Hooper said, *"That's enough – I have all that I'll need*
To go fishing, but I must get back with all speed.
Mr Holmes, in the morning I'll give you your hook -
If you bait it correctly, you might catch your crook."

THE PROMPT

Sherlock saw Lestrade's cab disappear as it moved
Through a street filled with fog and, at last, he approved
Of the way that he had been included, at last -
Soon, The Ripper would fall and belong to the past.

Both the friar and Watson retired to bed.
Alas, Holmes had to think, his great mind had been fed
And he had to digest all those thoughts running free
Through a brain which performed to a higher degree.

A pipe, perhaps two, and the thoughts which had raced
Would be put into order then properly placed
Into files in that attic he had in his head -
When needed, those files could be easily read.

On his sofa he puffed till those thoughts, one by one,
Had been filed correctly and, with this task done,
Sherlock Holmes drifted off to an overdue sleep,
A sleep which, indeed, was both dreamless and deep.

Mostly first to arise, Sherlock had to be shaken
By Watson who found that he had to awaken
His friend to advise him that he had missed dawn
And that, off for some fishing, they all had been drawn.

Watson held a newspaper in one hand while he
Shouted, *"Holmes, you must rise, for our hook has to be
Baited well if we're ever to capture our pike.
I will read Hooper's story to you if you like."*

"Was I sleeping?" asked Sherlock, surprised he had slept
In so deeply a manner while Hooper had kept
Up momentum ensuring the early edition
Had words to send Jack to a well-earned perdition.

"But go on, read it out," Sherlock asked of his friend,
  "Read it slowly from outset right up to its end
And then read it again – it's the hook we must bait
And to grab rod, reel and net, I admit I can't wait."

"I will," replied Watson, *"in good time, as you take*
Something into your body. And when you're awake
I will read it in full but, for now, breakfast well,
For today we must angle for someone from Hell."

"It says here, the Police have been contacted by
One of Jack's early victims who will testify
That, though wounded, she managed to make her escape
While Old Jack whimpered off hiding under his cape."

"But, Hooper, however, does not call him Jack
Or The Ripper, just someone who's made an attack
On some defenceless women alone in the night
But can't face men who'd probably put up a fight."

"Hooper goes on to say that it is to be hoped
That Police, though to date Scotland Yard hasn't coped,
Will be in a position, with what they have learned,
To checkmate this coward and give what he's earned."

"There's not much more to read, only that readers will,
In some later editions find out how the skill
And the pluck of a woman fought off someone who,
Upon meeting resistance, ran off like rats do."

Sherlock listened intently while munching on toast
And said, *"Well, it's a start, and I don't like to boast*
But I did tell Lestrade I should be on this case
Though I like fishing less than a good honest chase."

Watson countered by saying, "*You live in a dream.*
All of this, just admit, is the work of a team
Of which you are a part, a significant one.
Can't you ever acknowledge what others have done?"

"*The Police did the work but Lestrade had to wade*
Through a mountain of written reports which had made
Little sense due to fools making misleading claims.
Just who were these fools and just what were their aims?"

"*He was quite overwhelmed by a scale which would test*
Even you, Sherlock Holmes, even though you're the best
And most logical thinker there ever has been;
Though Lestrade, every day, on the job has been seen."

"*Don't forget Friar Geoffrey came down just as soon*
As he learned of events – the man has been a boon
And, together with what Mrs Sapper recalled,
And with Hooper's reporting – well, I am appalled."

"*Right, you are.*" agreed Sherlock, "*acknowledge, I must,*
All the efforts of others." and then threw the crust
Of his toast to his plate, "*Now, let's see if Lestrade*
And the team have put up an effective façade."

"*You're mixing your metaphors, Holmes, I declare.*"
Watson said with a grin, "*But I really don't care.*
Hooper's got the hook ready so, now, for the bait
And I'm sure for some fishing you hardly can wait."

"*Let the metaphors fall where they will, My Dear Friend.*
We must wait for the next few editions to wend
Their ways out to the Public and into Jack's hands."
Sherlock said in reply, "*we must watch the news stands.*"

"Should somebody respond to 'checkmate', it will take
Little time, I believe, for the letter to snake
Its way through to Lestrade – the Police have been told
They're to treat such a letter like it was of gold."

"Likewise, Hooper's editor sent an alert
That, a letter for 'checkmate', the staff should divert
To his desk without fail or any delay
And it would be despatched to the Yard right away."

"It's a waiting game, Watson; we cannot do more
Than we have up to now except hope that the score
Of Jack's victims stays put – we do not want more death.
But, till we see that letter, must I hold my breath?"

"You'll turn blue and expire." said Watson, "you loon,
For the mail will not come until mid-afternoon.
Read a book, play your fiddle or get some more sleep.
Don't go walking about – we have secrets to keep."

"The game is afoot and we must play our parts
And Lestrade will garrotte anybody who starts
Doing anything but that agreed on last night.
Do not get on the wrong side of him in a fight."

"Both the Sappers are gone – they are safe and secure.
We know Dot, Mrs Sapper, is ready to lure
Jack the Ripper as long as she is guaranteed
That the man is made pay for each dastardly deed."

"I am not very comfortable using poor Dot
As the bait on our hook, for it simply is not
The way I would have liked it, I'm forced to admit,
But she has insisted she must do her bit."

"Can we not get somebody to dress as she would?"
Friar Geoffrey broke in, *"For I would if I could*
But I fear I'm too tall and I wouldn't fool Jack
If he senses a hook, you will not get him back."

"She is small," Sherlock said, *"though her courage is huge,*
And it is as you say, that a failed subterfuge
Could be worse for it would send Old Jack off to hide
And a second deception, he would not abide."

"We'll get one chance to do this, and we dare not fail.
If we do, Dot may die and so every detail
Of our plan must be perfect." John Watson declared,
"I don't know about you two, but I'm rather scared."

"Not for me so much as for the one whom we risk,
So I hope we'll be ready to rush in to whisk
Out our bait from the jaws of this monstrous shark -
We should have this in mind well before we embark."

Sherlock then said to Watson, *"I'm told it's in hand.*
There'll be men posted out who will rush on demand
As the whistle is sounded – with guns they'll be armed
So, on that point, you shouldn't be greatly alarmed."

"Mrs Sapper, she says, will be armed with a knife
And is ready and willing to shorten the life
Of the one who attacked her, for those who have died
And herself, I expect. Her resolve has been tried."

There'd be hours to wait, half a full day, perhaps
Before there might come in any news, any scraps
Worthy of looking into – the day would be slow
But there may well be something it will have to show.

Both the friar and Watson had picked up a book
And suggested to Holmes that he might take a look
At the facts of the case he had gathered so far
For, to find a new clue, there was no one on par.

"Perhaps I'll read over the notes I have made
Just in case there's a clue managing to evade
Even my eagle eyes and enquiring mind -
Later on, I expect there'll be much more to find."

Sherlock took out his files and he went through his notes
Focussing in on the detail, the blatant misquotes
And the gross ambiguities which might direct
His remarkable mind to a telling effect.

He could see nothing more, nothing like a new clue,
So he put back the files and tried to subdue
Any urge to go off seeking facts for the case -
Like a hound chained and muzzled, he pined for the chase.

Baker Street had gone quiet, its tenants intent
To wait out Jack the Ripper until the man went
For the bait on their hook, they were biding their time;
In the meantime, Lestrade had a deskful of crime.

The Inspector went late to The Yard having spent
His time gathering up his preferred armament
Which his men would all bear when awaiting their prey -
He would say *"shoot to kill"* and his men would obey.

He'd go over the letters which came in the post
Though he knew that the letters would be, at the most,
From a Public of which Jack had made many cringe
But there would be a few from the 'idiot fringe'.

There was nothing to do but to sit down and wait
Hoping Jack read the paper and would take the bait
On the hook they prepared; he would hope it would not
Be inviting a letter from every crackpot.

He had yet to move into the New Scotland Yard;
It was under construction and ever so hard
To resist the temptation to put things on hold
Till the building was finished – a thing to behold.

But the criminals, sadly, would never comply
With requests to desist till he could occupy
That new building, brand-spanking, the state of the art
For the late Eighteen-hundreds, then crime could restart.

Jack the Ripper was one of a great many who
Lestrade had to investigate then attend to
When they'd been apprehended – his desk was awash
But the files kept on coming, the others they'd squash.

The first post came and went, there was nothing on chess
To be found in the letters, and none to be sent
To the trio at Baker Street eager for news -
Sherlock tensed up his muscles and stretched his sinews.

The second came, also, with nothing to show
But the second editions of papers would flow
With some more to be said on the woman who fought
And beat off her attacker – provoke Jack, it ought.

It was mid-afternoon when a letter arrived
At the newspaper office – its coming revived
An impatient Will Hooper who jumped up to say,
"This must go to Lestrade without fail, right away."

Hooper swung into action and hailed a cab
Yelling out, *"Scotland Yard – do not drive like a crab*
But speed off in great earnest – half a crown if I'm there
Just five minutes from now – set me down anywhere."

On his way, Hooper looked at the letter received
And knew well from its content he wasn't deceived -
This was from Jack the Ripper, no doubt about that -
They may not land a fish but they would snare a rat.

Scotland Yard was approached, Hooper readied to jump
Which he did coming down with an audible thump
On the footpath outside the old premises where
Two inspectors were seated, awaiting him there.

To the cabbie, he threw up the promised half-crown
Then he turned on his heels and began racing down
The long corridor seeking the men he must tell
That the ruse using 'checkmate' had gone off quite well.

Lestrade heard someone running – he jumped up to see
Who was in such a hurry and then, with some glee,
Gave a summoning yell for Gregson to *"Come quick.*
Hooper's here with some news – I hope it's not a trick."

Gregson came at a run to see what had been brought.
Was it good news or better, the news they had sought?
Back within Lestrade's office, formalities waved,
Hooper then handed over the letter they craved.

Lestrade read through it quickly – it said far too much
To be somebody's joke and he thought it, as such,
Was indeed from Old Jack – Hooper did himself proud.
Lestrade read it more slowly, again, and out loud.

"Don't believe," it began, *"what the papers have written*
Concerning a knight who, with 'checkmate', is smitten.
There had once been a pawn who was beaten by me
But refuses to fall – I cannot let this be."

"I had beaten that pawn – now she's raised to a queen
By her knights and a bishop. I see she has been
Whisked away to a castle with battlements high.
She should know that her death is both certain and nigh."

"For those knights cannot long save the life of the queen.
She'll get no royal quarter when trapped in between
The black knights who'll refuse any mercy. Instead,
They will give out a cheer as that queen topples, dead."

"There'll be no one to save her – she'll tumble away
And the king will hear 'checkmate' as death comes his way.
But we'll leave him in play till he sees his knights fall
And his bishop will suffer the worst death of all."

"He talks chess, we talk fishing, but it is my hope,"
Said Lestrade, *"that his game will end up with a rope*
'Round the neck of this fellow. Now we must advise
Sherlock Holmes of The Ripper's upcoming demise."

THE GAME

The three men walked on out – Lestrade called up a cab.
He looked back from the street and he saw just how drab
And depressing had gotten the Old Scotland Yard
"To get work done in this place is horribly hard."

"A great difference, I hope our new building will make.
It is long overdue but, then, all good things take
So much plotting and planning and lots of goodwill,
Not to mention the money the coffers must spill."

"You've brought light, Mr Hooper, into a dark place
And have shown us that we have a villain to face
In a very short while, I do earnestly hope.
It will be quite a story when Jack gets the rope."

"Well, we yet have to catch him but, if you have hope,
You have something which helps the despondent to cope
And to overcome all." William Hooper advised,
"If your man isn't taken, I would be surprised."

"But we now have to flush him from cover so he
Cannot hide in the shadows – that is up to me.
With my next little article I will suggest
Where the victim and bait, to look for, would be best."

"Well, it's you who can do it, if anyone can
For I cannot deny that our newspaper plan
Has drawn Jack out sufficiently that he'd express
His intention to win what he thinks will be chess."

"This, of course, will require a dangerous ploy
Using bait or, at least, a convincing decoy.
We must set things in motion; so pencil to paper -
Mr Hooper we need the next part of our caper."

"Our bait's at some risk, most especially when
She emerges from safety, away from our men
And the rest of her minders, so we must prepare
And keep Jack and his helpers, of traps, unaware."

"We shall trot off to Baker Street, there to alert
Sherlock Holmes, that inspired but annoying expert,
That the 'game is afoot' – it's his own call to arms.
Hooper, choose very well, for your words carry charms."

The three men were returning to Baker Street where
They would find an impatient trio waiting there
For some word that The Ripper was still playing chess,
Some word that the plotters were having success.

In the time that it took to traverse London's roads,
The three men pondered on the great evil which goads
Some to such heinous crimes that forgiveness could not
Be considered – damnation, alone, is their lot.

They also pondered that, if a man could play chess,
He could not be considered to be a brainless
And unfortunate product of abject neglect
And should have better things, to his mind, to direct.

"Was the man mean or mad?" was a question unasked.
When it came to the time that Old Jack was unmasked
He would go to the gallows, asylums were closed -
The 'black cap' of the court was already imposed.

The cabbie yelled out, *"Baker Street right ahead."*
And Lestrade told him that he should drop them instead
On the Marylebone Road – it was then a short walk
To the place where six men chose to gather to talk.

Mrs Hudson jumped up when she heard Lestrade ring
The doorbell of her Baker Street house – *"Do you bring*
Any news of the matters concerning that man?
I am not in your group but I'll help if I can."

"I can't tell you a thing, Mrs Hudson, I fear."
Said Lestrade with a wink, *"But I think it is clear*
You should bring us some coffee and food, for today
For a while we must be, from our beds, kept away."

"Go on up - I'll attend to such matters right now."
Mrs Hudson declared, feeling she was, somehow
And by more than a little, involved in the chase
And had her part to play in the Whitechapel case.

She felt she was in charge of maintaining those who,
Like a train's locomotive, at times, needed to
Be brought in to get water and load up with coal,
To be oiled and greased to proceed to its goal.

She provided the shelter whenever they came
From the tracks they had covered but, never, her name
Would be mentioned as part of the crime-fighting team -
Still, she always appeared bearing coffee and cream.

Was she taken for granted? Well, yes, but it's true
That, whenever her tenants were chasing some clue,
She was there taking care of the things they could not -
She'd not crave recognition, she kept the tea hot.

But nobody ignored her, they valued the care
That she took looking after the food she'd prepare,
How she maintained Two-twenty-one-B Baker Street,
How, at any odd hour, a client she'd greet.

The three men walked on in with a greeting, each one;
Mrs Hudson, her door-keeping duty now done,
Hurried back to her kitchen, her workshop no less,
There, the men's maintenance, to begin to address.

The greetings upstairs were both heartfelt and brief.
Lestrade said to the trio, *"It beggars belief*
But it seems Jack the Ripper is willing to play
For he's as much as said so on this very day."

Lestrade handed the letter to Hooper as he
Was, in every way, the main one who could be
Given most of the credit for prompting Old Jack
Into actions from which he might never come back.

"Well, you did write the article, Hooper, so now
You should read the response, then we'll figure out how
To procced from here on, how to make Jack come out
To the light where he'll find out what death is about."

As the letter was finished, Holmes said, *"If you please,*
Could you read it again but, this time, at your ease.
Pronounce every word but give none your own stress
For we must understand how he means to play chess."

Hooper read it again then did so one more time.
Sherlock sat back in silence, his truly sublime
Mind absorbing the message the letter contained.
"This isn't a challenge." the Great Sleuth maintained.

"It's a desperate act of defiance by one
Who's been shown to be able to be brought undone
By a woman, unarmed, but prepared to give fight.
Hooper, this letter gives me great delight."

"Mrs Sapper's the queen, that is patently clear
Gregson, Watson and I would all seem to appear
To be knights while Lestrade, I would say, is the king
Set for 'checkmate' – these words have a terminal ring."

"This is just supposition, I could be quite wrong
But the language Jack uses is lucid and strong.
His threat to kill all in that note is quite clear
And the bishop would be Friar Geoffrey, I fear."

"As I said, Jack's not mad, he's just evil and sly;
He enjoys what he does but he won't admit why.
Way deep down there's a man scared to find out that he
Cannot ever become what he thinks he should be."

"And what's that?" broke in Hooper, "The master of all?
The grand knight of old who sits upright and tall
On a charger defying the best in the land?
When Dot Sapper defied him, his feet turned to sand."

"In his mind, that's exactly where he sees his place
In the order of things – he refuses to face
The reality that he's a man, not a giant."
Answered Sherlock, "He's arrogant, always defiant."

"We must use this against him, it will keep him blind
To the trick we'll be playing – he'll be of a kind
Who will think we're the ones falling into his trap
And he won't know the truth till he hears ours go snap."

"We must lure him back to the scene of his crime
Against Dot where he'll hide, for the very last time,
In the shadows awaiting that queen who had fought
In a way that a queen, in at least my eyes, ought."

Hooper paused, then he said, *"I will let it be known*
That Scotland Yard's witness has now up and flown
Back to Whitechapel as she says Jack is a pawn
And, away from her home, she will never be drawn."

"I will quote her as saying 'there's work to be done
And she will not be kept from her home by someone
Who's too frightened to ever go forth in the light
And runs off if a victim can put up a fight'."

"I will use the word 'pawn' but I won't mention 'king'
Or, for that matter, 'bishop' or 'knight' - anything
Which may distract his mind from attacking the 'queen'
Or referring to chess I'll ensure won't be seen."

"In the early edition, this piece will appear
So Lestrade and his men have enough time to clear
The arena of battle of obstacles, large,
So when Jack does appear, in those men can all charge."

Lestrade ordered, at length, *"Enough talking for now.*
We know where, maybe when, and also who and how.
It is time to call 'Halt!' to these killings, gruesome,
So, the Sappers, from Henley to London, must come."

"There are many warehouses which Dot must go past
Walking home from her depot – she's always the last
To walk back – and it's here I expect that Old Jack
Would consider the best place to make his attack."

"It's quite dark and it's lonely, the street lights are dim,
Just the sort of a place that's ideal for him.
We can place men indoors, they'll be armed and alert
And, at taking down felons, they're very expert."

"We'll have more men in wagons not too far away,
Others spread through Whitechapel, he won't get away.
At all times, Mrs Sapper must keep near some light -
Anyone who approaches can be shot on sight."

The Sappers were summoned, Hooper started to write
Several draughts of an article phrased to incite
Jack the Ripper to action, to finish the job
He had started before – one more life he must rob.

Not much happened for days, no response was received
From The Ripper – Lestrade hoped he hadn't perceived
Any trap set to catch him; his men stayed in place
As Dot Sapper, her regular route, would retrace.

On the third night, all seemed much same as the first
And the second – perhaps Jack had lost any thirst
For the blood of more victims. The night would be long;
Lestrade was concerned things had gone badly wrong.

But Lestrade hadn't failed, The Ripper was set
To confront his first victim who'd managed to get
Right away from his clutches – the man was prepared;
He would do what no one had, before, ever dared.

There'd been investigations of places Jack might
Be sustained and supported but, as of that night,
No reports had come in of three habited men;
Lestrade considered this failure a sorry omen.

Jack had not sought out help, he would not do it tough;
He and both his disciples possessed quite enough
In resources to keep them in comfort and not
Being daily observed by some nosy abbot.

The three gathered that evening outside of the gate
Of an rundown old graveyard which no one of late
Had seen fit to maintain – it was Jack's favoured place.
It became his headquarters, his own evil space.

There were prayers to be spoken, attacks justified;
The foul place seemed to reflect the self-glorified
And delusional notion he had of himself.
Below ground, in a crypt, he kept 'things' on a shelf.

The three men had to push back a door rusted shut
Over so many years - it defied them all but,
They kept on till it gave and the darkness within
Seemed to summon them forward and bid them 'begin'.

In the depths of that crypt fully six centuries old,
In its deepest recesses, forsaken and cold,
Stood a robe-cladded form on a devilish frolic,
A chant on its lips of a form diabolic.

With that form were two more, a subservient pair -
They had been with their master and breathing the air
Full of foulness and death, their appearance the same -
They wore habits and hoods and were keen for the game.

In the crypt hung the trophies Jack took when he killed
All his victims, recalling the blood which he spilled
And the fear and the pain when each life was destroyed
With no thought of compassion or mercy employed.

Jack said, *"Now, my disciples, the time has arrived*
When that base harlot queen must, at last, be deprived
Of her life – I will send her to suffer and serve
Her great master in Hell – you must help not observe."

She walks home every evening about the same time
And tonight we'll attack – it will be a sublime
And magnificent moment – we'll all watch and gloat
As her blood rushes out after I've cut her throat.

Dot had started her walk, as she had now done twice,
Ever eager to do so till she could entice
Jack the Ripper out into the open to meet
His first victim, prepared and alert in the street.

Lestrade's men were all hidden, guns loaded, prepared
For whatever might happen; nobody had dared
Say a word in the darkness – Dot knocked as she went
By each way point to show Jack was not evident.

All at once, there was movement - a shadow was seen
Getting longer but fainter – something came between
Dot and where Lestrade stood, Gregson right by his side.
All at once, what it was seemed to stop and to hide.

Lestrade then grabbed his whistle preparing to blow
And alert everyone, should that shadow then show
That it was from somebody out stalking poor Dot.
That 'somebody', he hoped, wasn't some drunken sot.

Two figures then moved – they were stealthy, the pair,
And they moved toward Dot who, indeed, had a fair
Idea that she was stalked by someone in the street -
She could hear the faint sound of some pattering feet.

Sherlock saw them move too, he was hiding with Ben
To rush in to support Lestrade's well prepared men.
Lestrade saw one advance – he was hooded and looked
To be holding a knife – it would seem Jack was hooked.

Lestrade blew on his whistle as hard as he might
And his men ran from cover out into a night
Which was dark all except for the lamplights' dim beams -
Dot reacted at once to her husband's loud screams.

Ben rushed in to help Dot just as soon as he saw
That someone was approaching – he struck at the jaw
Of the closest attacker, the other just turned
To escape – it seemed, the attack, he had spurned.

He was stopped by another, Watson raised his gun
As did Gregson – they told him if he chose to run
He'd end up being shot in the street where he stood;
He stopped, raised his hands – the man had understood.

Lestrade's men rushed on in, Watson's man was detained,
The one who'd been struck, laying still, had remained.
But where was the third? Could that man be Old Jack?
He appeared and advanced in a frenzied attack.

But he didn't get far – with the butt of a gun
He was given a blow on the head which would stun
And stop him in his tracks – Dot appeared safe and sound
When the first to go down bounded up from the ground.

In his hand was a knife – he grabbed Dot by the arm
And intended to do her some devilish harm.
He had caught her off-guard but she still pulled away -
This disciple, it seemed, was determined she'd pay.

But Ben was nearby and he struck out once more
At the jaw of the man he had put down before.
The man staggered but still had the knife in his hand
And the power to strike was still his to command.

Friar Geoffrey looked over and saw Dot and Ben
Had confronted the man but he raced over when
He could see, as the hood from his face was pulled back,
He was not a disciple, this man was Old Jack!

THE KILL

The Good Friar rushed in but was stabbed in the arm;
There was blood on his habit although little harm
Had been actually done – Dot was then face to face
Once again with the killer – she hadn't much space.

Her knife she had pulled from her jacket then swore
She was willing to die or to kill him before
She would let him kill any more women that way;
Dot was very determined to make the man pay.

Ben grabbed Dot and he pulled her away from Old Jack
But, in doing so, he had exposed his broad back;
Jack lunged with his knife next to Ben's shoulder blade,
But, in doing so, he lost the tool of his trade.

Holmes and Watson were running as fast as they could
To reach Whitechapel Jack – if they lost him, he would
Take revenge against any and all he would meet -
But, for now, he was unarmed, exposed in the street.

Two men had been stabbed, they were hurt but alive;
The friar was bleeding but he would survive.
However, protruding from Ben Sapper's back,
Was a knife – Watson had to call off his attack.

Holmes was ten yards away when he saw Jack had spun
Right around and that he was now starting to run.
"Do not let him escape." he said under his breath,
"If you do, it will lead to more mayhem and death."

Jack, however, was loose and was getting away
But then Dot with a yell and a scream blocked his way.
He was unarmed and frantic – he ran right at Dot
But she just stood her ground putting Jack on the spot.

He believed he could push her away for he thought
That this woman he faced was so small that she ought
To be frightened so much she would faint on the spot
But his insides would soon get a message from Dot.

Dot's knife pierced his belly then upward she ripped
With its razor-sharp edge and, as quickly, she slipped
It out from his intestines – Jack screamed for dear life.
Dot said, *"Take that and like it – I'm Ben Sapper's wife."*

"It's a woman who's taken you down, you disease,
So just lay there and scream as you die – it would please
Every woman in London to see you this night -
There'll be great celebrations because of your plight."

"Say your prayers, Friar Jack, I will laugh as you die
And send you off to Hell with no word of a lie.
You're pathetic, you coward, now beg as you bleed -
I will not lose a minute of sleep for this deed."

"Friar Geoffrey and Ben have been hurt, that is true,
But they are of a sort which is hard to subdue
And will live many years, while your carcase we'll toss
Somewhere too good for pigs – to us, you'll be no loss."

Watson looked up and saw it was Whitechapel Jack
Writhing 'round in the gutter but, still, from the back
Of Ben Sapper protruded a knife which he must
Remove now, though the wound wasn't fatal, he'd trust.

He had one other patient - Friar Geoffrey said, "*No!*
Ben's hurt far more than I and to him you should go.
Fix up Mr Sapper and then you should try
To keep Old Jack alive, though you might ask me why."

Watson said to the friar, "*Your wound, I must treat*
Or you'll lose too much blood; but this cut is so neat
That the wound can be sealed until I can get
You stitched up good and tight – you'll recover, I'll bet."

"*Next, I'll treat Mr Sapper – his wound isn't deep*
And has cut into flesh, so his life he will keep
Which I don't think is true for that man in the street -
I do fear that, his maker, Old Jack will soon meet."

"*There's no chance for The Ripper, I see that from here*
But I know that the words which you speak are sincere.
I must save who I can but decisions are tough
And Old Jack has found justice can be rather rough."

Sherlock came back to help his friend Watson but found,
Although wounded, the two men were sorry but sound
And would have to be stitched; Friar Geoffrey said, "*Now*
We must tend to the dying – we must help somehow."

"*Please take this to him, Sherlock; he may yet have time*
To admit what his done, each and every crime,
And may beg for forgiveness before it's too late.
He will soon meet his maker who'll seal his fate."

Sherlock said, *"Yes, of course. You're a good man and true*
But The Ripper, I know, will get what he is due."
From the hand of the friar, he took what he could tell
Was a crucifix, small, one which had been worn well.

"That cross used to be his but he left it behind."
Said the friar, *"There still might be time to remind*
Him of what life should be and the debt that is owed
From the time our first heartbeat is ever bestowed."

The Sleuth ran to where Dot was still holding the knife
Which she used to remind Jack the Ripper that life
Must be paid for, in full; then he knelt to return
The old cross which Jack once had decided to spurn.

Sherlock said, *"You should hold this."* but he couldn't tell
If the man was still breathing or if the death-knell
Had been sounded for Whitechapel Jack, so he placed
The old crucifix onto the breast it once graced.

Dot said, *"You're a bit late - to the Devil he's gone,*
And I'd say that the sun in the sky never shone
On a less worthy man than this scum in the street -
Satan's face is the next countenance he will greet."

"I did that less for Jack than for one who I know
To be better than I – he refuses to crow
At the death of this monster, the one we've all killed."
Explained Holmes, *"He is one who'll not say he is thrilled."*

Lestrade came up running, his pistol was cocked
And his gaze, onto Jack on the ground, had been locked;
"It seems I'm too late, someone else got our man
But we have his two helpers locked up in the van."

"It was me who has gutted The Ripper, this night,
And I don't care who knows it – not much of a fight
For the pig was unarmed and was running away."
Dot declared, *"I suppose you will take me away."*

"It's a medal you'll get and the whole nation's thanks
And a massive reward you can take to the banks
If I have any influence down at The Yard."
The Inspector replied, *"All those worries, discard."*

"I can tell you that, as I'm in charge of the case
And as I was involved in the ruse and the chase
After Whitechapel Jack and you feared for your life,
You defended yourself rather well with your knife."

"That's how it will read, my report which I'll write,
Though it will be touched up to make it more polite
When I speak of the way that this man stabbed two men;
He was frantic and filled with the full strength of ten."

"It was we, Scotland Yard, who came up with the plan
Which would put you in danger – we did get our man
With the help of a woman who had to step in.
How to thank her? I wouldn't know where to begin."

Without fuss, Lestrade said he would have Jack removed
For, if word got about, he would not have approved
Of the way people might have behaved when they found
Jack the Ripper was there, lying dead on the ground.

He'd be torn limb from limb in an orgy of hate
And, being dressed as a friar, a terrible spate
Of religious outrage might ensue which could end
With attacks on the clergy one could not defend.

And the man was a Lord, not a great one, but still
He was listed as noble, a Noble who'd kill
And defile in a most callous manner those who
Had no means of defence and no one to turn to.

Lestrade called up a wagon; four men picked up Jack
From the road where he lay and threw him on the back
And then covered the body – the Inspector explained,
"To leave the man here cannot be entertained."

"There'd be riots and burning across the whole land.
Revolutionary fervour would grow and expand
Till we couldn't supply any firm guarantee
That the Queen and her family would not have to flee."

"Quite right." said a voice from the darkness, *"We shan't*
Let such things come to be; it is something we can't
Ever countenance happening – empires might fall,
Most especially ours - we can't have that, at all."

"Mycroft!" shouted Sherlock, *"We don't need you now.*
We did ask for your help but you seemed to, somehow,
Always find an excuse that you could not assist.
You had men on the ground we hoped we could enlist."

Mycroft entered the lamplight and said, *"Brother, mine.*
I am glad you're not injured, I couldn't decline
The temptation to come out to see how you'd fare
On the streets of Whitechapel – I really do care."

"But I'm not a policeman and can't interfere
In the day to day problems of Scotland Yard's sphere
Of involvement. But did you believe I did not
Keep a very close eye on the help Lestrade got?"

162

"We observed Mr Hooper attend Baker Street;
Gregson and Lestrade were permitted to meet
With both you and the Doctor, although you were struck
From the Yard's list of experts – that wasn't just luck."

"We were there on the bridge when the Sappers arrived;
We were listening in as the group had contrived
A quite workable plan – but, if Whitechapel Jack
Showed his face, he'd be snaffled and not given back."

"We, that is I, down at Whitehall knew well
That The Yard, with your help, would be able to tell
Fact from fanciful fiction when letters were read -
That business of chess proved a definite thread."

"It was there all along, that remarkable clue,
And The Yard in its wisdom might yell and argue
That it should have been seen and then acted upon
But, the words 'should have seen' aren't in my lexicon."

"Lestrade needed more eyes, ones like yours, that I knew,
So I took it upon myself, then, to renew
My contacts with those persons well-placed in The Yard -
I said, 'You need my brother, don't make things so hard'."

"But your fame went before you, they valued the way
That what took them a month you could do in a day.
But, when things got reported, Watson had the knack
Of depicting the Force as inept and quite slack."

"It took some persuasion to make them agree
That Inspector Lestrade should go off and be free
With the records, official, with you and your friends -
I had to ensure it would pay dividends."

"This will all go away, all this Whitechapel mess,
Though I fear that some people, especially the Press,
Want to keep it alive but, in time, I would bet,
Jack the Ripper, the monster, we all will forget."

"His two henchmen, or friars, or monks or whatever,
Will both, I assure you, be taken and never
Again walk about in the bright light of day -
In the deepest of dungeons we'll lock them away."

"That's a punishment for them and also the way
That we'll guarantee that they will not get away
And tell any and all the true name of Old Jack
For, from where they're both going, nobody comes back."

"Dr Watson, you especially must understand,
There is more here at stake and I have to command
You to put down your pen and have nothing to say
About Whitechapel Jack and events of this day."

"This is not a request but a rigid decree
From the highest office of the land. You'll agree
To abide by this edict or risk the displeasure
Of they who hold power too potent to measure."

"If that sounds like a threat, I'm afraid that it is.
You are Sherlock's good friend but, alas, even his
Tongue is silenced forever, his pen had been stilled,
We do not want folks knowing who's really been killed."

"The newspaper's been paid off and told to resist
The temptation to print, but we had to insist.
Hooper doesn't yet know this – he will be advised
He won't like it but we cannot be compromised."

"Now, the Sappers cannot be allowed to just walk
From this place and feel free to discuss things or talk
To the Press, so we'll offer an ample incentive -
I'm sure, in this case, we can be quite inventive."

"Mr Sapper," said Watson, *"needs medical care*
As does Friar Geoffrey. You should be aware
That they both have been injured – you cannot hide that.
They've been stabbed by your favourite aristocrat."

"Their wounds are not fatal but, treat them, we must
So, as Jack is quite dead, I'd suggest that you just
Get right out of our way – there are things we must do
And, a hospital, they must be now taken to."

Mycroft said, *"That's in hand. There's a carriage nearby.*
We can't trust London Hospital's staff to comply
With our sensitive needs - to the Barracks we'll send
Your two wounded and they'll soon both be on the mend."

"You may go along with them – your clearance is good
For your military service, it is understood,
Leaves you with, though on leave and receiving half pay,
A commitment to act and to do what we say."

"Of course I'll go with them." said Watson, annoyed
At the actions of Mycroft, *"They both were deployed*
In the face of great danger – I'll not leave them now
But the pair must be treated somewhere and somehow."

"Mrs Sapper goes with me, on that I'll insist,
While you'll just, I presume, go back into the mist
Out of which you'd emerged far too late for the fight.
Like Old Jack, you like shadows and stay out of sight."

"Out of sight, Dr Watson, but not out of reach."
Countered Mycroft, *"Never! But does history not teach*
Us that war must be staged in a disciplined way -
Some must stand back till needed, not jump in the fray."

"I cannot have my men attend every crime
Even though they'd be able to much of the time.
They are specialised tools of a secretive trade
And the limelight is something they have to evade."

"But when we were advised, by those secretive tools,
That our Ripper, assisted by two other fools,
Was a Peer of the Realm who felt free to kill those
Of the lowest estate, a dilemma arose."

"If it ever got out that our man was a Lord
Then the masses of London would take up the sword
And make war on the order we all now enjoy.
It was time, we decided, those tools to employ."

"But, Lestrade is a capable man, as you know,
Even though you depict him as witless and slow.
With those stories you write, have you never surmised
That to take all the credit could be ill-advised?"

"Perhaps you, Dr Watson, should ponder upon
What might have been prevented if Sherlock was on
The Yard's list of consultants? It was he who saw 'chess'
As the clue which eventually brought this success."

"Without my intervention and very good luck
Brought to bear by a friar with admirable pluck,
You would never have seen any files about Jack.
Those lives lost between times – we can't get them back."

"We must limit the damage and hope for the best
So the memory of Jack the Ripper will rest
For all time as the passions in people decrease
And their memories of his depravity cease."

Mycroft did what he could; no one knew Jack had been
Gutted right in the street and nobody had seen
Or reported a death. Watson had to agree
To keep silent – it was an official decree.

Though this stuck in his craw, he accepted the ban
Taking solace in that he had helped stop the man
Who held London in terror – five women had died,
Perhaps more, but with silence, John Watson complied.

Sherlock Holmes lost all interest – a new case arose
Which required the use of that sensitive nose
To sniff out an offender who no one else could.
Friar Geoffrey, to go back to Yell, said he would.

It was anti-climactic - The Ripper was dead;
Sherlock Holmes had a case to distract him instead;
The Sappers were happy; Hooper was content;
Lestrade into New Scotland Yard had been sent.

Watson looked out his window one drizzly day
And he said to his friend, *"Well, it won't go away,*
The true story, untold, of how evil was swept
From the streets of Whitechapel while everyone slept."

Sherlock looked at his friend, took a puff on his pipe
And said, *"Watson, you know that it's past time to wipe*
From you memory, the matters on which you now dwell.
It is only a story, and one you can't tell."

"In your mind is an attic, more cluttered than mine,
And, if keeping it tidy, you simply decline
The next story you start out to write will be one
Which, because of that clutter, will never get done."

"Get a broom and a duster and sweep your mind clear
Of those facts you don't need - make them all disappear
For you have much to write and so much you might share
And a mind, like a desk, to begin, should be bare."

"Watson, My Dear Friend, I do think we may say
That the streets of old London are safer today.
And while quite a good story's a thing you may lack,
Jack the Ripper's forgotten and will not come back."

....

Also from Allan Mitchell

Sherlock Holmes and The Menacing Moors

A call from an old comrade has Holmes chasing a reported agent of Satan between the towering tors and bottomless bogs of Dartmoor only to find the limits of his own confidence and his Public's esteem. Only Watson stands his friend but even his patience is stretched. Sherlock's retreat to the bees of Sussex serves only to show him that his skills are unique and are desperately needed elsewhere. On returning to London, Holmes finds malign forces have been bringing ridicule to his doorstep. In this tale, the Great Sleuth is brought to life, uniquely, in expressive verse, a favourite form of the author who loves the language of Sherlock Holmes and the Menacing Moors.

Also from Allan Mitchell

Sherlock Holmes and The Menacing Metropolis

More Menacing than the Menacing Moors, the Great Metropolis harbours evil and deviltry far more sinister than Dartmoor could offer - it is not for nothing that Watson describes London as the great cesspool draining the Empire of its dregs. Its evil stems from the hearts of the most heartless of men, evil against which a group of stalwart Londoners is determined to act. Knowledge is power and forewarned is forearmed, it is said, but fore-knowledge is fragile and Sherlock must balance probability with instinct, caution with decisiveness, when warned of impending disaster for both City and Realm. Allan Mitchell's stirring stanzas of reeling rhyme once again stretch back to an earlier era to witness the never-ending battle between Sherlock Holmes and the Menacing Metropolis.

Also from Allan Mitchell

Sherlock Holmes and The Menacing Melbournian

Burgeoning, brash and bold, a new Metropolis has burst forth from the golden soil of Terra Australis, proclaiming its virtues but harbouring many of the evils of old which have been attracted by fortunes won from the Earth itself. Shadowy figures menacingly emerge from distant wars to deprive the unwitting of that which has been earned by honest toil. One such figure wends its way across continents to stake a much larger claim on a much older Metropolis to help establish a kingdom of fear and domination. Resolutely, relentlessly, our deerstalker-decked detective must once more rhythmically rhyme his way along a perilous path fighting forces of evil, evil which refuses to be quelled but is known to him and his forthright companion as the Menacing Melbournian.

Also from MX Publishing

MX Publishing is the world's largest specialist Sherlock Holmes publisher, with over a hundred titles and fifty authors creating the latest in Sherlock Holmes fiction and non-fiction.

From traditional short stories and novels to travel guides and quiz books, MX Publishing cater for all Holmes fans.

The collection includes leading titles such as _Benedict Cumberbatch In Transition_ and _The Norwood Author_ which won the 2011 Howlett Award (Sherlock Holmes Book of the Year).

MX Publishing also has one of the largest communities of Holmes fans on Facebook with regular contributions from dozens of authors.

www.mxpublishing.com

Also from MX Publishing

Our bestselling short story collections 'Lost Stories of Sherlock Holmes', 'The Outstanding Mysteries of Sherlock Holmes', 'Untold Adventures of Sherlock Holmes' (and the sequel 'Studies in Legacy') and 'Sherlock Holmes in Pursuit'.

www.mxpublishing.com

Also from MX Publishing

Sherlock Holmes Re-Imagined

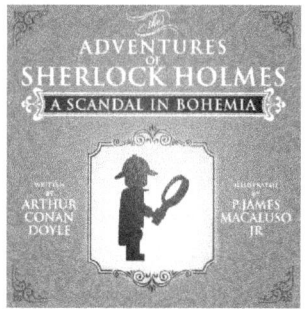 

Twelve original adventures from Sir Arthur Conan Doyle,

re-illustrated in Lego.

In this book series, the short stories comprising The Adventures of Sherlock Holmes have been amusingly illustrated using only Lego® brand minifigures and bricks. The illustrations recreate, through custom designed Lego models, the composition of the black and white drawings by Sidney Paget that accompanied the original publication of these adventures appearing in The Strand Magazine from July 1891 to June 1892.

www.mxpublishing.com

Also from MX Publishing

"Phil Growick's, 'The Secret Journal of Dr Watson', is an adventure which takes place in the latter part of Holmes and Watson's lives. They are entrusted by HM Government (although not officially) and the King no less to undertake a rescue mission to save the Romanovs, Russia's Royal family from a grisly end at the hand of the Bolsheviks. There is a wealth of detail in the story but not so much as would detract us from the enjoyment of the story. Espionage, counter-espionage, the ace of spies himself, double-agents, double-crossers...all these flit across the pages in a realistic and exciting way. All the characters are extremely well-drawn and Mr Growick, most importantly, does not falter with a very good ear for Holmesian dialogue indeed. Highly recommended. A five-star effort."

The Baker Street Society

www.mxpublishing.com

www.ingramcontent.com/pod-product-compliance
Lightning Source LLC
Chambersburg PA
CBHW071601200626
46811CB00027BA/860